M000305518

SEAL JUSTICE

BROTHERHOOD PROTECTORS

NEW YORK TIMES BESTSELLING AUTHOR
ELLE JAMES

Dedicated to my family. I love them all so very much and value their support and kindness. Hug your loved ones today.
Elle James

AUTHOR'S NOTE

Visit ellejames.com for titles and release dates
and join Elle James's Newsletter

CHAPTER 1

REGGIE MCDONALD HELD her breath and listened for him. She shivered, her naked body chilled by the cool damp air of her prison. Though her brain was murky, her thoughts unclear, and her strength diminished, she knew what she had to do. When she could hear no sounds of boots on the wooden steps leading down into the earthen cellar, she continued digging. Inch by inch, she scraped away at the soil of her cell, praying she was correct in assuming hers was on the edge of the group of cells. If she dug long enough, she might see daylight and find a way to escape the hell she'd been trapped in for what felt like a lifetime.

Using the tin cup she'd been given to drink from, she scooped dirt from the corner behind the door. That small space was hidden from her captor when he came to feed her or shackle her to take her up to the big house where he tortured her and the other young women he'd kidnapped and held in the horrible dungeon beneath his house.

If she got out, she'd find help to get the other women out and save them from the sociopath who forced them to bow to his bidding. If they didn't do what he said, he whipped them with a riding crop or shocked them with a cattle prod. Sometimes, he burned them with the lit end of the cigars he smoked.

To keep them pliant to his will, he drugged their food and water, making them weak and groggy, unable to form clear thoughts or fight back.

Reggie had caught on to what he'd been doing. She couldn't quit eating or drinking completely, but she'd skip a day and use that time of semi-clear thinking to work through the problem to come up with a solution. On those clear days, she'd acted just as drugged when she'd been shackled and taken up the wooden stairs to the Master's house. When she could see out a window, she'd determined the house sat on the side of a hill, the slope dipping downward from the back of the structure. Though the women were trapped in the cellar, the earthen walls of their prison couldn't be that thick, especially on the far end where she was being kept. The hill sloped sharply on that end, giving her hope that, with steady digging, she'd eventually break free of captivity and escape.

Reggie prayed she was correct and scooped faster, pushing the soil she'd dislodged into the sides of the walls and floor, packing it down so that her captor couldn't tell it was fresh dirt.

She paused again as a sound penetrated the wooden door of her cell.

Footsteps.

"He's coming," a voice whispered. Reggie recognized Terri's voice. She was in the first cell, closest to the stairs. She'd been there the longest. A single mother of a little girl, she'd held out all those days, suffering through the torture in hope of seeing her little girl again. Lately, she'd fallen into despair of ever escaping.

Quiet sobs sounded from other cells along the row.

Reggie emptied her cup, quickly patted the dirt she'd removed into the ground, dragged her tattered blanket over her naked body and moved to the opposite corner where she curled up and pretended to be asleep.

Boots clunked down the steps to the bottom.

Silence reigned, even the few sobs ceased as the women held their breath, praying the Master wouldn't choose them for the trip up the stairs.

Reggie waited, listening. When a door hinge creaked, she braced herself.

"Please, no. Please," a woman's voice pleaded with the Master. It was Beth, a young college student who'd been captured on her way home from a night class. "Don't hurt me," she cried.

"Shut up and move," the Master's harsh voice echoed in the darkness.

"No, please. I can't." The sharp crackle of electricity sparking was followed by a scream.

Reggie winced and bit down hard on her tongue to keep from yelling at the man for hurting Beth. She couldn't draw attention to herself. Not now. Not when the hole she'd been digging was already two feet wide and as deep. If he took Beth up to the house, he'd be distracted long enough Reggie might finally break through.

Beth cried as she stumbled up the stairs, the Master's footsteps sounding as he climbed up behind her.

As soon as the door clicked closed at the top of the stairs, Reggie grabbed her cup and went back to work, digging furiously, scraping the dirt away with the cup and her fingernails. The Master usually kept a woman up in the big house for at least an hour before he brought her back to her cell. She didn't have much time.

She abandoned quiet for speed and dug as fast as she could.

"What are you doing?" Terri whispered, her voice barely carrying above the scraping sound of the cup on dirt and rocks.

Reggie ignored her, determined to get as far as she could before the Master returned.

Her cup struck a large rock. Undeterred, she

scraped around the edges, her heart beating faster, her breath coming in ragged gasps. The drugs in her body slowed her down, making her want to crawl into her blanket and sleep. But she couldn't.

"Stop whatever you're doing," Terri said.

Reggie halted and listened. When she didn't hear footsteps or the quiet sobs of Beth being returned to her cell, she went back to work on digging around the rock.

Soon, she found the edge of one end of the stone and worked her way around it.

After scraping and digging for what felt like an hour, she poked through the dirt and felt cool, fresh air streaming through a tiny hole onto her fingertips.

Not trusting her hands, she pushed her head through the tunnel and sniffed fresh air, the scent of decaying foliage a welcome scent from the earthen cell. She inhaled deeply, her breath catching on a sob. She'd been right. Her cell was on the edge of the hill. If she dug a little more, she might be able to push through. The large rock was in the way. If only...

She pulled her head out of the tunnel and shoved her bare feet in and pushed as hard as she could.

The rock didn't move.

Lying on her back, the cool dirt floor making her shiver, she scooted closer, bunched her legs and kicked hard with her heels, over and over until the rock moved. Hope blossomed in her chest and gave her the strength to keep pushing and kicking.

"You have to stop," Terri said. "When one of us crosses him, he punishes us all."

Another one of the women sobbed. "Please don't make him mad."

Reggie didn't want any of them to be hurt by her actions, but the Master was hurting them every time he took one of them up into the house. She had to get out and get help for all of them. Using every last bit of her strength to kick and shove at the boulder until it rocked and gave, she finally pushed it free of the soil, and it rolled down the hill. Loose dirt fell into the tunnel, blocking the sweet scent of fresh air.

Using her feet again, Reggie pushed at the dirt. More fell into the gap. She scrambled around and shoved her arms through the tight tunnel and patted the loose dirt against the walls of the tunnel, shoving the excess out and down the hill.

"Shh!" Someone said from one of the other cells. "He's coming."

A door opened above them. Sobs sounded as Beth descended into her prison, followed by the clumping sound of the Master's boots.

Reggie hadn't taken the time to pat the dirt into the walls this time. If the Master came into her cell, he'd catch her at digging her way out. She looked through the hole. Gray beckoned her. She shoved her shoulders through the tunnel. It was tight. Really tight. But if she could get her shoulders through, she could get the rest of her body through. Desperately inching and wiggling her way inside, she prayed she could breach the exit before the Master jerked open her door, grabbed her by the ankles and yanked her back inside. He'd beat her and chain her. And he'd throw her into the wooden box beneath the stairs where he kept the "naughty" girls.

No way. She couldn't let that happen. Not when she could taste freedom.

With her body blocking the tunnel, sounds of weeping and cries were muffled. Reggie couldn't tell if the women were informing the Master of her scratching and digging. She wasn't sticking around to find out. Once her shoulders were free, she braced her hands on the edges of the hole and pushed as hard as she could. Her body scraped through until her hips were free of the tunnel. Grabbing onto nearby branches, she pulled her legs out of the hole. Once all of her was free, gravity took hold, and she tumbled down the hill, her skin torn and gouged by sticks, rocks and bramble.

The jabs and tears made her cry out with joy. The pain wasn't inflicted by the Master but delivered by nature as a testament she was out of that hell.

She came to a stop when her head hit the big rock she'd pushed free of her tunnel. For a long moment, she lay still, her vision blurring, pain raking through the base of her skull.

Then she heard the sounds of dogs barking, and her heart froze. The Master had two vicious looking

Rottweilers he'd kept tethered when he'd brought her up into the big house.

Reggie staggered to her bare feet and shivered. The cool night air wrapped around her naked body. Swallowing the sobs rising up her throat, she ran, following the hill downward. She didn't know where she was or which way to go, only that she had to get as far away from the house and the dogs as possible. She hadn't come this far to be ripped apart by his maniacal dogs or dragged back to house and beaten until she couldn't remember who she was or why she cared.

Sticks and rocks dug into the soft pads of her feet, drawing blood. She kept running until her feet were as numb as her skin and mind. The dogs were getting closer. She had to do something to lose them.

The hill continued downward. A cloud crossed over the sky, blocking what little starlight penetrated the tree branches. Her lungs burning and her heart beating so fast she thought it might explode out of her chest, Reggie was forced to stop long enough for the cloud to shift, allowing the starlight to illuminate her way.

When it did, she stared out at a dark canyon. She stood on the edge of a precipice. Easing to the edge, she could see the glint of starlight off what appeared to be a river forty feet below where she stood.

The barking dogs were close now.

Reggie turned right then left. No matter which

way she went, the cliffs were still as high as the one in front of her. She couldn't backtrack. The dogs were so close enough, they'd find her.

She refused to give up. But what else could she do? Die from the vicious rendering of sharp Rottweiler teeth, go back willingly to the Master's house to be beaten, or jump off a cliff into water of which she had no idea of the depth?

When the barking sounded right behind her, Reggie spun to face the two Rottweilers, emerging from the tree line...stalking her.

A shout from behind them made her heart leap into her throat. The Master.

Without further thought or mental debate, Reggie turned and threw herself over the cliff.

As she plunged downward, she steeled herself for the impact against rocks or whatever lay beneath the water's surface.

Crossing her arms over her chest, pointed her toes and hit the river feet-first, sinking deep. The chill shocked her body, but she kept her mouth shut tight, and struggled, kicking hard to rise. Just when she thought she would never breathe again, she bobbed to the surface and gasped. Above her, she heard the wild barking of the Rottweilers.

The cold water helped clear her foggy brain. She had to make the Master think she was dead. Taking a deep breath, she lay over, face-first in the water and floated as far as she could before turning her head to the side to take another breath. She did this for as long as she could hear the dogs barking above. The Master had to think she'd died in the fall from the cliff. It was the only way to get away and make him think she couldn't tell the authorities about what he had hidden in his basement.

After a while, the sound of the dogs barking faded. Knowing the dogs couldn't follow her scent in the water, she let the river's current carry her along as she treaded water to keep her head above the surface.

The cold sapped what little energy she had left. She rolled onto her back and floated into the shallows where she dragged herself up onto the shore.

Darkness surrounded her, embraced her and sucked her under. As she faded into unconsciousness, her last thought was...*I'm free.*

CHAPTER 2

"WELL, Talon, welcome to the Brotherhood Protectors." Hank Patterson held out his hand with a grin. "Glad to have you aboard."

Sam "Talon" Franklin held out his hand to his new boss. "Thanks, Hank, for having faith in my abilities. I hope I live up to your expectations."

"If I didn't think you could do the job, I wouldn't have hired you," Hank said. "You being a Navy SEAL, I know you have the key ingredients necessary to take on any assignment that might come your way with the Brotherhood Protectors. We can always use a weapons expert who's also good at hand-to-hand combat. I think you'll fit right into the team. Flexibility and being able to take charge in difficult situations will come in handy in this job, as it did in your SEAL days. No matter the mission, you're up for the challenge." He shook his head. "We get all kinds of assignments. Some more exciting than others."

"I look forward to my first mission," Sam said. "I guess I should go by Sam, now that I'm no longer a part of the Navy SEALs."

"Noted." Hank nodded. "I'm looking through our most recent requests. I'll have something for you by the time you come back from your fishing trip." He glanced around the little cabin. "Will this old hunting cabin be enough for you and your dog until you can find more suitable accommodations?"

"It's perfect. Small enough it won't take me much time to clean. It has a bed, which always beats the cold hard ground, electricity, a refrigerator and heat. Most importantly...it's off the beaten path, so I'll have all the privacy and quiet Grunt and I can stand." Sam grinned. "Tell your wife we appreciate her finding it for us. It'll work out fine."

"Sadie likes to help out when she's on hiatus from her work. She's in the middle of a two-month break and getting a little stir-crazy."

"I've seen some of her movies. She's really talented," Sam said. "Don't you get jealous when she kisses other actors?"

Hank nodded. "Like mad. But she always comes home to me and Emma. I know how much she loves me, and I love her more than life itself."

Sam's chest tightened. He'd pretty much given up

hope of ever finding that kind of love. It just wasn't in the cards for him.

"Enough about me and my family. You have a vacation to start." He pulled a device out of the bag he'd carried into the cabin. "We finally got satellite phones. Cellphone coverage can be non-existent out here. Swede, our computer guy, will man the satellite phone while in the office. If you need to get hold of me, he'll pass on the message. But you won't need this until you start work. Now, go." Hank waved toward the door. "Sadie filled the small pantry with some canned foods, stocked the refrigerator and freezer with meats, vegetables, milk, juice and beer. And she put clean sheets on the bed for you when you get back from your fishing trip."

Sam shook his head. "Remind me to thank her. She went way above and beyond anything I could have expected."

"We wanted you to have a smooth transition to your new job and life. If you need anything, all you have to do is ask."

"Thanks," Sam said. "I appreciate all you've done for me."

Hank clapped his hands together. "Did you get with the outfitter I told you to try?"

With a nod, Sam stepped out of the cabin onto the porch. "I did. He fitted me out with all the paraphernalia associated with fly fishing. Now, I just have to remember how to do it."

"There's no science to it. Just do what feels natural." Hank chuckled. "The fish don't always follow the rules anyway."

"Are you sure you don't need me for the next week?" Sam asked, half-hoping Hank would put him right to work.

"Nope. Go. Enjoy your leave. We'll have you working before you know it." Hank clapped a hand onto Sam's back. "See ya in a week." He climbed into his truck and left Sam standing on the porch.

Sam wasn't sure how to relax. Being on his own for an entire week without anyone shouting, shooting or harassing him, even if good-naturedly, would be a new experience. One he wasn't certain he was equipped to handle. Already, he missed his brothers in arms, the only family he'd known for the past eleven years, and he wondered if he'd made the right decision to leave the Navy and join the civilian world.

He left the cabin Sadie had found for him and drove up into the Crazy Mountains, following the directions the outfitter had given him to the river he'd recommended for fly fishing.

Once there, he unloaded his gear from his truck and looked around. The light green of the grassy glen contrasted sharply with the dark green branches of Lodgepole pines climbing up the hillside. The river in front of him was shallow and meandering through an idyllic valley. Instead of making him relax, the quiet and emptiness of the landscape made his shoulders tense. What if he got bored? What if he found he couldn't stand to be alone? What if he wasn't any good at civilian life? Would the Navy take him back?

Sam slipped into his waders and pulled them up to his waist like the man in the outfitter store had shown him. He gathered his fly fishing pole, the lures he'd purchased, and then let Grunt out of the back seat of his pickup.

The sable-colored German Shepherd leaped to the ground and ran a circle around the truck before he tore off into the brush.

"Grunt!" Sam called out. He wasn't quite sure the dog knew to stick around. They'd only been together for three days since he'd arranged to adopt the retired military war dog. He'd picked him up from San Antonio, Texas before he'd begun the long trek to Eagle Rock, Montana, where he'd met his new boss, Hank Patterson, former Navy SEAL and entrepreneur.

The two men had known each other from having served in Afghanistan several years ago. Sam had heard about Hank's new venture in protective services. In a corps as small and close-knit as the Navy SEALs, word got around.

When Sam had decided it was time to leave the Navy, he'd contacted Hank, hoping he had room for one more highly trained combatant. He promised he could be retrained to provide protection to those who needed it and could even live with the cold temperatures found in the Crazy Mountains of Montana.

Hank assured him that he had room for more good men in his agency, the Brotherhood Protectors. All Sam had to do was get to Eagle Rock, Montana.

He had arrived that day, met with Hank and gotten the low down on what was expected. Because he was still on terminal leave, he wanted to postpone his actual start date until he'd had a chance to unwind from his last mission.

His fingers tightened on the fishing pole as the events of that final mission came back to him in waves of anger, regret and grief. Pushing thoughts of the men who hadn't been lucky enough to return home on their own two feet and the civilians who'd been caught in the crossfire, Sam baited his hook with a fancy lure, walked out into the middle of the shallow river and cast his line out the way the outfitter had taught him.

He flicked the line, dragging the lure across the water and willed the tension out of his shoulders. He was supposed to be relaxing and unwinding from active duty. The new job wouldn't start for another week, giving him the time he needed to adjust to civilian life. No uniforms, no rank, no one shooting at him. Life would be very different. No surprises. How hard could being a bodyguard be?

A loud splash in the water behind him made Sam

jump. He spun and crouched in a combative position, ready to take on the enemy.

Grunt bounded through the water, came to a stop beside Sam and promptly shook the water from his fur, spraying Sam where he'd planned on staying dry. "Hey, shake somewhere away from me."

As if he understood Sam, Grunt took off for the riverbank and sniffed through the reeds until he disappeared into the brush. Sam shook his head. Grunt had seemed so happy to be rescued from his kennel. The dog had jumped up into Sam's arms and slathered him with sloppy kisses. He remembered him from when they'd been together in Afghanistan, before the last mission. Sergeant Tyler Bledsoe, his handler, had been killed when a Taliban rebel had tossed a grenade down the narrow alley they'd been sent into. The dog and the handler had been hit by shrapnel. Sgt. Bledsoe's protective vest hadn't saved him. He'd taken a hit to his neck, severing his carotid artery. He'd bled out before anyone could do anything to slow the bleeding.

Grunt had lost an eye and was laid up with shrapnel wounds. Thankfully, he hadn't been put down on the spot. He'd been evacuated back to the States with other human casualties aboard a C-17 equipped with a critical care team to Germany. A veterinarian cleaned out the shrapnel and arranged for the dog to be transported back to Lackland Air

Force Base, where he'd been officially retired and put up for adoption.

That mission had been Sam's last before he'd separated from the Navy a month later. He'd followed Grunt's progress and expressed his desire to adopt the animal once he'd been released from active duty. He'd felt he owed it to Grunt's handler to give the dog a home.

The least he could do for Sgt. Bledsoe was take care of the dog that had meant as much to him as any other member of his family and give him a forever home in his retirement. Grunt had served well, saving the lives of so many soldiers, SEALs and Delta Force. He deserved a good life.

Sam cast the line out again, trying to get the hang of fly fishing, scooting the lure across the water again.

Grunt barked...not something he did often. The sound drew Sam's attention away from his fishing.

About that time, something hit the lure and dragged the line down.

Grunt's barking became more insistent, almost desperate.

With a fish on his line, Sam hesitated. The outfitter in Bozeman had warned him that the mountains and streams in the area were inhabited by bears. He should be looking out for them while he fished.

Grunt continued barking, the sound getting louder.

Sam waded back to shore, tossed aside his expensive fly-fishing pole and tromped along the river bank toward the sound.

He saw Grunt before he saw the source of his distress.

Sam pulled his handgun from the holster beneath his jacket and wondered if a bullet from a 9 millimeter pistol would slow a bear long enough for him to get Grunt to safety. Or would it just piss him off?

Though he searched the brush beyond Grunt, Sam couldn't see a bear. And the dog wasn't barking upward at a bear but into the brush bordering the river.

His gun drawn and ready, Sam approached, wondering if Grunt had cornered another animal.

Flicking the safety off, he edged toward Grunt. As he neared the dog, he noticed the bank sloped sharply down to a grass-covered sandy beach between him and Grunt. Something pale and smooth lay among the grass and reeds.

As Sam got closer, he realized it was a body. A naked body. Beyond the body, Grunt stood, the ruff on the back of his neck standing at attention. In front of Grunt, was a wolf, standing in the shadows of the brush, crouching low, ready to spring.

Sam pointed his gun into the air and fired one shot.

The wolf bolted, ducking into the woods.

Once the wolf was gone, Grunt backed toward the body and sniffed.

Sam scrambled down the slope and hurried to the inert form, lying naked in the sand. As he closed the distance, he could tell by the shape of the hips, it was a woman, lying face down in the sand.

At first, he couldn't tell if she was breathing.

He knelt beside her and felt for a pulse at the base of her throat. He couldn't quite tell if he had his fingers in the right place since she was lying face down. He was hesitant to move her in case she'd suffered spinal injuries. But if she wasn't dead, she'd die soon enough from exposure. Gently, he rolled her over and touched his fingers to the base of her throat. His breath lodged in his throat, and he prayed for a sign of life.

Just as he felt a faint pulse, the woman moaned, and her eyelids slowly lifted.

She stared up at him, her eyes widening. Then she slapped at his hands and kicked her feet in a pathetic attempt to fight him off. She was too weak to escape his hold.

"Hey, I'm not going to hurt you." He let go of her long enough to strip off his jacket and lay it over her naked body, trying not to notice her breasts, the tuft of hair at the juncture of her thighs and how perfectly formed she was, even though her skin was bruised and scratched, and her feet looked like hamburger meat. She had to have been running through the woods to get that beat up.

"We need to get you to a hospital." He scooped her up and straightened to stand.

She tried again to fight free of him, but he only held her tighter. "It's okay. You've been injured. I'm going to get you to a doctor."

"No," she whispered.

He frowned down at her. "No, you weren't injured?"

"No doctor," she said.

"At least let me contact the police. You had to have been running from someone to get all these injuries."

"No doctor. No police." She shook her head. As if that little bit of effort was too much for her, she passed out in his arms.

"Well, damn." Sam trudged along the river and headed back to his truck. He opened the back door and laid the woman on the bench seat. Then he stripped out of his waders, threw them into the back of the truck. He didn't want to waste time retrieving his fishing pole. If it was there when he got back, good. If not…oh well. He held open the driver's door. "Grunt. Up."

The dog flew into the seat, over the console and onto the passenger side.

Sam climbed into the truck and turned in his seat

to stare at the woman lying unmoving. Every instinct told him to get her to a hospital as quickly as possible. And to have them run a rape kit on her. Someone had probably kidnapped, raped her and dumped her body. Whoever had done that needed to be caught and prosecuted. Hell, he needed to be shot.

Anyone who could abuse a woman and leave her naked and exposed to wild animals and the elements deserved a bullet through his black heart.

But the woman had specifically said no doctor and no police.

Why?

And what was he supposed to do with her if he couldn't take her to the hospital or to the police?

"I'm taking you to my boss," he said out loud.

"No," she croaked.

He turned in his seat to see she was looking at him, pulling his jacket over her nakedness.

She opened startlingly green eyes as if it took all her strength to do so. "I can't be seen."

Sam shook his head. "I have to get you some help."

She moaned and reached out her hand. "No. Please."

"I don't understand." He stared into her gaze. "You need help."

"No one can know I'm alive," she said. "I have to stay...dead." Her eyes closed and her voice faded off on the last word as if she'd truly died.

Sam fought the urge to climb into the back seat

and start CPR. For a long moment, he stared at the jacket resting over her breasts, willing it to move.

When it did with the rise of her chest, Sam let go of the air arrested in his own lungs.

Hell, if she wouldn't let him take her to a hospital, the police or his boss, he had to do something to make sure she didn't die on him. He shifted into drive and pulled back onto the dirt road he'd come in on. Minutes later, he was on the highway heading to the cabin Sadie and Hank had rented for him. It was the only place he could think of where he could take her without her protesting.

He turned up the heat in the cab of the pickup. How long the woman had been exposed to the elements, he didn't know, but she had to be kept warm until he could get her somewhere safe and dry.

Thirty minutes later, he pulled up to the little cabin in the woods. He dropped down from the driver's seat.

Grunt leaped to the ground beside him.

Sam yanked open the back door and stared at the woman, wishing he'd gone with his first instinct. She needed to go to the hospital.

She lay with her eyes closed, the jacket having slipped down, exposing the rounded curve of a breast with a rosy nipple, puckered against the cold.

He slipped his arms beneath her, lifted her out of the back of the truck and carried her into the small cabin, against his better judgment.

Thank God, Hank's wife had stocked the cabin with sheets, towels and pantry goods. Sam hadn't thought that far ahead, preferring to get straight to his vacation and the alone-time he'd needed to decompress.

He hadn't had more than a couple hours by himself before he'd found the woman. So much for decompressing in peace and quiet.

Sam laid her on top of the hand-sewn quilt Sadie had draped across the bed. His jacket slipped off her body, exposing how scratched and bruised she was. He couldn't lay her between the sheets like that, but he didn't feel right cleaning her up. Hell, he didn't know her, and he didn't have her permission.

But she was unconscious. The wounds would get infected if he didn't clean and dress them. His training in the Navy had taught him self-aid and buddy care. He just had to think of her as one of his teammates and get the job done.

He located his duffel bag and pulled out his handy first-aid kit. After locating a washcloth, a large bowl and filling it with warm soapy water, he went to work on cleaning up the woman and dressing her wounds with antiseptic ointment and bandages. She lay almost comatose while he worked, gently wiping away the dirt, mud and blood. When he was finished, he dressed her in one of his clean T-shirts and slipped her between the sheets.

Grunt sat beside the bed and laid his chin on the

quilt, his gaze shifting from the woman to Sam. The dog whined softly.

"I know. We should have taken her to the hospital," he whispered, patting Grunt's head. "She could have internal injuries from a fall."

As he stood there, he fought the urge to shake her awake. If she didn't have brain damage or internal injuries, sleep would be the best elixir on the path to getting her back on her feet.

As he waited for her to wake, he shoved a hand through his hair and shook his head, the enormity of what had happened hitting him square in the gut. Holy hell, how had he ended up with a naked, unconscious woman on his vacation? He was supposed to be relaxing and finding his footing in the civilian world. The way things were going thus far, civilian life might be every bit as dangerous as his military world.

CHAPTER 3

THE SCENT of something cooking tugged at Reggie's empty belly. Warmth wrapped around her and made her want to keep her eyes closed to continue sleeping. However, her stomach rumbled and ached, finally forcing her to open her eyes and seek the source of the enticing smell.

For a moment, she couldn't focus. Something dark and damp was in front of her, but she couldn't make it out in the dim light.

She pulled her blanket up around her, only it wasn't her blanket, and she wasn't naked beneath it. The dark damp thing in front of her moved and breathed hot breath on her face.

Reggie jerked backward with a muffled cry. Tangled in fresh, clean sheets, she couldn't roll to her feet. Instead, she fell hard onto a wooden floor, jolting her insides and shooting pain through the hip on which she landed.

The animal leaped up onto the mattress above her and stared down at her, his tongue lolling and his tail wagging. She realized it wasn't a wolf, but it was another kind of canine that could inflict a lot of damage if he was trained to do so.

"Grunt, *platz*," a firm, deep, male voice sounded from somewhere on the other side of the bed.

Reggie fought to free her legs from the sheet and scooted into the corner of the room, as far as she could get away from the animal and his master.

The Master.

A terrified shiver rippled across every inch of Reggie's skin. Where was she? Had the Master gotten a new dog? Had all her efforts to escape landed her back in the hands of the man who'd kidnapped her and other women? She searched the immediate area around her for a potential weapon but found none. Her fingernails were broken and stubby from digging. She was weak with hunger and the lingering effects of the drugs the Master had fed her. But she'd rather die than go back to the torture and abuse at that madman's hands. If she had to, she'd kill the bastard to get away.

"Hey," the voice said from the end of the bed. A man appeared, dressed in jeans, a black T-shirt and bare feet. "Are you okay?"

She stared at him. Was he the Master? Had the

Master removed his mask and taken on a different tactic to gain her trust and cooperation before he destroyed it and beat her into submission?

"Need help getting back into the bed?" The man had dark hair and brown eyes. He didn't look like a sociopath. But then she hadn't met another sociopath until the Master. And though he wore a mask when he took the women up into the big house, he couldn't hide his steely gray eyes that showed no emotion until they were sparked with anger.

"Take my hand. I'll help you up." The man held out his hand.

Though she was convinced this man wasn't the Master, Reggie wasn't sure it was safe to trust him. He could be working with the Master to kidnap women.

He moved closer. "You need to get back in the bed. It's supposed to get down below freezing tonight. You'll want to conserve your strength."

She shrank back even more, pulling his T-shirt down over her legs, her body shaking. "Are you going to rape me?"

His eyes widened. "Hell, no. And I'm not the one who put those bruises, cuts and scratches on you." He shook his head. "Look, lady, I could have left you in that river to be eaten by a wolf or bear, or you could have died from exposure. If you hadn't protested so adamantly, I would have dropped you at the nearest hospital and been done with my good Samaritan act.

Now, are you going to let me help you? Or are you going to die anyway?"

Even through her fuzzy head, she could tell he was impatient with her. Reggie frowned. "Not much of a bedside manner," she mumbled.

"Not much of a patient," he shot back. He held out his hand without moving closer. If she wanted his help, she'd have to meet him halfway.

After what she'd been through at the hands of her captor, she wasn't ready to trust any man.

Then her rescuer's voice softened. "Look, I don't want to hurt you. I've had more than enough opportunity, if I did. I'm on vacation and just want to be left alone. The sooner you're well, the sooner you're out of here, and I can get back to my solitude."

She stared into his eyes and then her gaze shifted to his hand. Finally, she reached out and laid her fingers against his palm.

The man closed his hand around hers and gently pulled her to her feet.

His hand was cool and dry. As soon as she was upright, her head spun, the room dimmed, and she lost all control of her muscles. She sank into a black abyss.

IF SAM HADN'T CAUGHT her, she'd have fallen on the floor. He lifted her in his arms and swore.

Her body was on fire.

He laid her on the bed and hurried to wet a cloth with the cool mountain water from the tap. From what Hank had told him, the water was from a well that tapped into a spring. Cool, refreshing and just what the woman needed to bring down her fever.

He carried the cloth to the bed and placed it on her brow.

The woman moaned but didn't open her eyes.

Grunt stood beside Sam and rested his chin on the bed. His gaze shifted from Sam to the woman. He let out a soft whining sound.

"It's okay," he said. "She's going to be all right."

He pulled one of the kitchen chairs up beside the bed and sat with her for the next hour, rewetting the cloth and applying it to her forehead, her neck and cheeks. The longer her fever lasted, the more concerned he became. She could die if he didn't take her to a doctor.

Grunt held vigil as well, refusing to lie down for the first hour. Finally, he curled up beside the bed and slept fitfully, waking up every few minutes and lifting his head to look at Sam, as if asking how the patient was doing.

After two hours with no break in her fever, she lay completely still and unresponsive.

Worried, Sam picked up the satellite phone Hank had left.

The woman didn't want anyone to know she was alive. No hospitals, no police. Hell, that tied his hands when he didn't know who she was or if she had family who could come to her rescue. The only other person he knew who lived close enough to help was Hank Patterson, his new boss.

He entered the number Hank had given him with the phone and pressed send. If he didn't do something to help the woman, she could die.

Not on his watch.

Hank answered the phone immediately. "Sam, I thought you were out fishing and camping?"

"I was, but I've got a situation." He went on to explain about Grunt finding the woman, and how she'd begged him not to take her to a hospital or the police. "She's burning up. If I don't do something soon, she'll die. I don't have anything to give her to bring the fever down. Cool compresses aren't touching it. I can't leave her to go to a pharmacy. What I'm telling you is that I need help, but it needs to be discreet."

"On it. I'll have someone there in the next thirty to forty-five minutes." Hank ended the call.

Sam set the phone on the kitchen table and returned to the bed.

The cool compress he'd laid across her head had fallen onto the pillow, leaving a damp spot.

Her head rolled from side to side, her brow puckered. "No," she whispered. "Don't hurt them."

Sam leaned closer, hoping to learn more about this stranger. He didn't even know her name.

"Don't hurt who?" he asked softly.

"Don't hurt..." she said, her voice fading.

"Who are you?" he asked, shifting the cloth back to her forehead.

"Dead," she murmured. "Must be dead..."

"What's your name?" he asked.

"Dead." She tossed her head a couple more times, and then lay as still as death. Her cheeks were flushed a ruddy red and were covered in a sheen of perspiration.

He had to get her cooled off or the fever would fry her brain.

Sam lifted her into his arms and carried her into the small shower. Turning on the water, he stood holding her in his arms as the water sprayed over both of them, drenching their clothing and skin.

She struggled weakly, but not enough that he feared he'd drop her. She was in no shape to fight back. And he had to get her body temperature down.

After five minutes in the shower, the color in her cheeks had returned to a more normal peachy pink. The T-shirt he'd dressed her in was soaked and lay plastered against her skin, revealing the beaded peaks of her nipples and the rounded swell of her breasts.

When she shivered violently, he switched off the water, hooked a towel with his fingers and stepped out of the shower onto the floor mat. He tried to stand her on her feet so that he could dry her body, but she kept sliding down his front.

Giving up, he scooped her into his arms and carried her back to the bed, laying her on the hastily spread towel.

He grabbed another towel from the small bathroom and dried her as best he could. Digging another of his T-shirts out of his duffel bag, he pulled the damp one over her head and dressed her again in a dry shirt.

He'd just finished tucking her beneath the sheet when a hard knock sounded on his door.

Sam stiffened. He glanced from the woman on the bed to the door and back. The only person who knew she was there was Hank.

He took his gun out of the holster he'd hung on a hook on the wall and crossed to the door. "Who's there?"

"Sam, it's me, Hank."

"Are you alone?" Sam asked.

Hank hesitated. "No. I brought Sadie. She worked as a medical assistant in a hospital before she made it to the big screen. Let us in. We can help."

Sam unlocked the door and edged it open.

The sky had darkened to a steely gray. The sun had settled behind the Crazy Mountains, leaving the land cloaked in the dusk before dark.

Hank stood before him, his wife, Sadie, beside him, her hands covered in oven mitts, holding a container.

"We brought chicken noodle soup and some

medicines that should help to bring down the fever," Sadie said.

Sam stepped aside.

Sadie entered, followed by Hank.

Sam peered into the growing darkness for a moment before he closed the door and twisted the lock.

"Who's watching Emma?" he asked.

Sadie shot a smile over her shoulder as she laid the pot of chicken soup on the small kitchen counter. "Chuck and Kate were visiting when Hank got the call. They stayed to babysit Emma."

Sam frowned. "You told them?"

"Not that you had a woman up here," Hank assured him. "Only that a friend was ill, and we needed to help. Chuck and Kate were happy to stay. Their little girl, Lyla, loves Emma. Now that Emma is walking, the two of them are all over the place." She held out her hand for the bag Hank was carrying.

He handed it to her and glanced at the bed. "How long has she been out?"

"I found her about four hours ago. She's been out most of that time. She came to briefly, got out of the bed and promptly passed out again. Her body is hot. I put her in the shower to cool her off, but that didn't wake her."

Sadie ran a digital thermometer over the woman's forehead and shook her head. She stared at the reading and shook her head. "She's running a 104 degree temperature." Sadie turned to Sam. "She needs to be taken to the hospital."

Sam drew in a deep breath and let it out. "When she was lucid, she was adamant. No hospital and no police. I didn't know where else to take her."

Sadie set the thermometer aside and held out her hands for the satchel Hank had carried in. After she dug through the contents, she pulled out a bottle of pills. "She's not going to die, if I have anything to say about it. Help me sit her up. We have to get these into her to help reduce the fever."

Sam hurried forward and helped brace the woman in an upright, seated position on the bed. He held his arm around her shoulders and spoke to her. "Hey, you need to wake up and take some medicine."

She moaned and shook her head.

"Please," he said. "We need to bring your fever down. Come on, open up." He rubbed his thumb across her cheek.

The woman leaned into him and opened her mouth enough for Sadie to push two pills between her teeth and hold a bottle of water with a straw up to her lips.

"Drink," Sam ordered.

For a moment, she didn't move, but then she sucked the water up through the straw and swallowed, and then swallowed again and again.

When Sadie tried to take away the bottle, the

semi-conscious woman reached out and grasped Sadie's hands, bottle and all, and kept drinking.

Sam's heart constricted. The woman was ravenously thirsty. He took one of her hands and squeezed gently. "Slow down, sweetheart. You can have more in a little bit."

Sadie took the water away.

The woman on the bed moaned, her head rocking back and forth.

"It's okay. We'll take care of you," Sam said. "We won't let anything bad happen to you."

"What do you think happened to her?"

"Based on the scratches and bruises, she's been running from something or someone," Sam said. "Or she was dumped in the river to die. Since she was naked, I'd bet sexual abuse is not out of the question." His teeth ground at the thought. In his opinion, any person who sexually abused another should be shot. Studies had proven those kinds of people were sick and couldn't be rehabilitated.

"Hey, sweetie." Sadie applied a cool compress to the woman's forehead. "Can you tell me your name?"

Again, the woman moaned and tossed her head right and left.

Sadie shook her head. "She needs to be at a hospital. If the fever doesn't come down soon, you should take her, whether she likes it or not."

The woman shot up into a sitting position, her

eyes wide and bloodshot. "No. I have to be dead. He'll kill them."

When she started to slump back, Sam sat on the side of the bed and held her in the upright position. "Who is he?"

She looked at him as if she didn't quite see him and whispered, "The Master." Then her body went limp against him.

Sam looked to Hank. "The Master?"

Hank frowned. "She's running a high fever. She could be hallucinating. Even if she'd named a name, we couldn't be sure it was a correct name. But *The Master*... I have no idea who she's talking about. Could be the guy who left her to die in the river."

Sam eased the woman back until she lay against the mattress. He retrieved the cool compress that had fallen onto the pillow and placed it across her forehead. "It would help if you could tell us your name," he whispered. He didn't like calling her *the woman*.

Sadie stood with her hands on her hips. "She needs to be at the hospital. If she's been raped, they need to run a rape kit on her."

"I know that, but you saw her." Sam nodded toward the unconscious woman. "She's adamant."

"What do you think she meant by she has to be dead or he'll kill them?" Sadie asked.

Hank's frown deepened. "Could be that whoever had her has others. If they think she's alive, she might lead them back to him. He might kill the others and dump the bodies before the police can catch up to him."

Sam's fists clenched. "Is there any way we can search for her face among reported missing persons?"

"I can have Swede tap into facial recognition software and see if we can come up with a match." Hank pulled out his cellphone and snapped a photo of the face of the woman lying in the bed.

"I wish we knew her name," Sadie said. "It would be much easier to find her family and let them know she's alive." She glanced up at Sam. "She wouldn't be, if you hadn't found her in the river."

"I didn't find her," Sam said. He nodded toward Grunt. "He did."

Grunt had moved up beside the bed and laid his chin on the mattress, stretching his neck so he could sniff the lady lying so very still. He whined and looked up to Sam.

Hank smiled. "I think he knows she's not well."

"Yeah. He's been by her side since he found her."

"I've found dogs to be a good judge of character." Hank held out his hand to his wife.

Sam snorted softly. "Even characters who happen to be comatose?"

Sadie took her husband's hand, her gaze going to the dog and the woman. "I'm leaving you some warm soup. When she comes to, she'll be hungry. The soup will be a good start to filling her empty belly. I can come back tomorrow with a casserole, if you like." She met Sam's gaze with a hopeful one of her own.

"You've done a good job of stocking the pantry and refrigerator with food. I've been on my own for years. I can rustle up some grub, when necessary."

"We'll stop by tomorrow, anyway," Hank said. "To check on her progress."

"I'd stay, but—" Sadie started.

"No, really, I can handle it from here," Sam said. "You've got a little one to go home to."

"You know, I have half a mind to ask Mia Chastain to come out. She's a rape survivor. If your lady has been assaulted, she'd be a good resource and a shoulder to lean on during her recovery." Hank turned to Sam. "Bear Parker's one of my recruits from Delta Force. He's a good guy. Mia's an award-winning screenwriter. She's amazing."

Sam held up a hand. "I appreciate that, but until I know what she's afraid of, I don't want too many people knowing about her. You heard her, she insists on playing dead. And maybe that's the best thing we can do for her until she can tell us why."

Hank and Sadie both nodded.

"Let us know what you find out," Hank said. "And congratulations. This can be your official first case as a Brotherhood Protector." He held out his hand to Sam.

Sam gripped Hank's hand and shook on it.

"Thanks. I couldn't take on anything else until I know what's going on with her."

Sadie touched her husband's arm. "We'd better get back before Chuck runs out of patience with Emma." She grimaced toward Sam. "Now that she's mobile, she's a handful." Her grimace morphed into a joyful smile. "I never knew how much work and how much fun a baby would be."

Hank laid a hand on the small of his wife's back. "She's all that and more." He gave a chin lift to Sam. "I expect to hear from you with any changes to her condition. In the meantime," he held up his cellphone, "I'll have Swede run that facial recognition software and see if we get a match on the missing persons databases."

"Thank you." Sam hated to see them go, but at the same time, he was glad when they did. Once their truck left the yard, he returned to sit beside the bed and removed the damp cloth on her forehead. After wetting it and wringing it out with cool clean water, he leaned over her, placing the cloth over her brow and whispered, "Hurry and get better so we can get whoever did this to you."

CHAPTER 4

REGGIE BLINKED OPEN her eyes and stared up at wooden beams rising at a steep angle to the apex of a vaulted ceiling. Those beams weren't the plain two-by-fours that had been the flat ceiling of her earthen-walled cell.

A soft light burned from a lamp on an end table, spreading a golden glow over the corner of a small room. The scent of wood smoke gave her a feeling of warmth and security like she hadn't felt in a while. Her hands moved, her fingers touching smooth sheets and soft jersey covering her body.

Sniffing sounds next to her ear made her turn sharply.

A black snout lay beside her. Before she could scream, a long, wet tongue snaked out and swiped her chin.

Reggie jerked away. A squeal shot up her dry throat, coming out as more of a croak.

A face appeared over her.

Fear ripped through her, paralyzing her.

"Hey," a deep, resonant voice said. His warm, minty breath brushed across her face.

A hand holding a cup with a straw moved into her view.

"Thirsty?" he asked and held the straw to her lips.

She shook her head.

"It's just water," he insisted.

And whatever drug he'd decided to add to it. She shook her head again and stared at him through narrowed eyes. "Who are you?" The words came out as a whisper. Her dry throat disallowed any real sound from making it past her vocal cords.

"My name is Talon. Er...Sam Franklin." He smiled. "What's your name?"

"Reggie McDonald," she answered automatically. Her eyes narrowed even more. Were those the eyes behind the masked man who'd kidnapped her and held her captive for so long? The voice didn't fit, but she wasn't completely clear-headed. "Talon?"

He shrugged. "That's the nickname they gave me in BUD/S training.

She shook her head, trying to clear the lingering fog. "You lost me."

"BUD/S. Basic Underwater Demolition/SEAL

training. I'm a Navy SEAL." He cleared his throat. "Or I was. I left active duty a few days ago."

She wasn't sure she believed him, though he looked sincere. "Where am I?" she said, continuing to whisper.

"In my cabin, outside of Eagle Rock."

The black-nosed animal slipped beneath the man's elbow and lay on the bed beside her.

The man smiled and rubbed a hand over the dog's head. "This is Grunt, also recently released from active duty. You can thank him for finding you."

She stared at the dog. He had one bright black eye. A jagged scar sliced over the dog's face and his other eye. That eyelid was forever closed, appearing to be sewn shut. "Does he bite?" she asked, forcing the words past her vocal cords, tired of whispering. The croaking sound was worse.

"Please, drink this. You've had a fever. The liquid will help your body recover from it." He held the cup and straw toward her again.

She shrank back. "How do I know it's not drugged?"

His brow formed a V. "Drugged?" He looked down at the cup. "Why would I drug you?" When he glanced back up, his frown deepened. "Is that what happened to you? Someone drugged you?"

She nodded.

He put his lips to the straw and drank from it. "There. If it's drugged, I'll be drugged too."

She stared at the cup again, her mouth so dry she felt as if Death Valley had taken up residence on her tongue.

"Look, if I'd wanted to hurt you," he said. "I could have done it while you were out for the past twenty-four hours." He shoved the cup in front of her. "If you like, you can have Grunt taste it, too. I promise, it's just water."

She tried to sit up but fell back against the pillow.

Talon set the cup on the nightstand, slipped an arm around her and helped her into a sitting position, stacking several pillows behind her then laying her back against them.

Once she was positioned, he handed her the cup.

She held it for several seconds. The water inside looked so wet and inviting she couldn't resist another moment. Reggie drank until the cup was empty, and sucking through the straw made a loud, empty sound.

Talon, or Sam, chuckled. "Want more?"

She wiped her hand across her mouth. Her lips were chapped, and her hand shook. She realized she was weaker than she thought. For a moment, she closed her eyes and let the water settle in her empty belly. "What do you want with me?"

He laughed. "To get you well enough to tell me what the heck happened. And now that you're my assignment, I need to see that it doesn't happen again."

44

"Assignment?" She shook her head and lifted her eyelids. "What do you mean…assignment?"

"I just started working for an organization called the Brotherhood Protectors. My boss, Hank Patterson, and I are former Navy SEALs. He hired me to do personal security work. You know, like bodyguard, private investigation, or whatever is needed." He raised his hands, palms up. "Since I found you in the river, he's taken your case and assigned me to figure it out. That is, if you want me to help."

Her head spun. "Look, Talon—Sam—whoever you are, how do I know you don't work for him?"

"Call me Sam," he said. "By *him*, I assume you're referring to *The Master*?"

Her eyes rounded, and that fear rippled through her again, making her cold all over. "You know him?"

Shaking his head, Sam pulled the sheet and a quilt up over her. "No, but you mentioned him when you were delirious with fever. Is he the one who hurt you?"

She nodded.

"Do you know who he is?" Sam asked.

She shook her head. "No. He wore a mask. I never saw his face."

Sam frowned. "That will make it more difficult to track him down."

"Why would you help me?" She pinched the bridge of her nose. "You don't even know me."

"Well, for one, my boss just made you my assignment." He glanced down at the dog. "And Grunt likes you. I'm told dogs are good judges of character." He scratched behind the German Shepherd's ear. "Right, Grunt?"

"Grunt?" She snorted softly. "That's his name?"

The dog barked, startling her, sending a shiver of terror through her. She shrank away from Grunt. A flash of déjà vu rippled across her memory. Dogs had barked as they'd chased her to the edge of a cliff.

Sam touched the dog's head. "Grunt," he said in a stern voice. To her, he said, "Are you okay? Grunt didn't mean to scare you."

"No," she said, holding up her hand. "He d-didn't s-scare me," she lied. "It's just..." Reggie swallowed hard with her suddenly dry throat. "Could I have more water?"

He hurried to the faucet in the kitchenette on the other side of the one-room cabin, filled the cup and returned, handing her the cup and straw.

She drank, thinking back over what had happened that had led to him finding her in the river. As she remembered, the terror of her escape washed over her. She trembled all over, and her hand shook so hard, she spilled water on the quilt.

Sam took the cup from her and set it on the nightstand. "Hey, it's okay. You're safe here."

When she continued to shake, he eased over to sit on the bed beside her and pulled her into his arms. "I promise, I won't hurt you. And I won't let anyone else hurt you."

He held her stiff body for a long moment. When she didn't relax, he leaned back and looked into her eyes. "Is my holding you making you uncomfortable? If it is, I'll let go." He shifted his body, loosening his hold around her.

She shook her head and leaned into him. "No. It's just… Oh, sweet Jesus. I'm free. I can't believe I got away." All the horror of captivity threatened to overwhelm her. The trembling increased until she realized she was crying. Sobs wracked her body and left her wrung out and weak.

The arms around her were loose enough she could get away easily, but strong enough to make her feel protected for the first time since she'd been abducted.

Sam smoothed back her hair from her forehead and held her until she ran out of tears. Still, she leaned against him, soaking up his warmth and strength. When she finally pulled away, the cool air made her shiver.

"I'm sorry," she said, wiping her damp cheeks with the back of her hand.

"No need to be." He shifted back to the chair beside the bed and waited for her to pull herself together. "When you're ready, could you tell me what happened and why you want to be dead?"

She nodded, gathering her breath and the courage

to share what she'd gone through. She had to. If she wanted to get the others out, she had to accept help. From what Sam had told her, he was there to help her. The women still being held captive needed help if they were to be freed, and soon. Before the Master discovered she hadn't died in the fall over the cliff into the river. That didn't give her much time to find him and the women he held captive below his house.

Only problem was, she didn't know who he was. How could she find the man if she didn't know his name and hadn't seen his face? She'd been taken to his house unconscious, and she wasn't sure how far downstream she'd gone before she'd washed ashore. She wasn't even sure if she'd traversed one river or multiple rivers before she'd been discovered by Grunt and Sam.

All she knew was that she had to find the others and free them before the Master killed them. And he would, if he thought she was alive and looking for him.

She leaned back against the pillow and closed her eyes for a moment, wondering how much she should tell Sam and how much she could leave out. What she'd been subjected to was demoralizing and dehumanizing. For the sake of the others, Reggie couldn't hold back what she had to say. If Sam was to help her, he had to know what kind of monster had held her captive.

. . .

Sam waited patiently for Reggie to open up and tell him what had happened that had led her naked, bruised and scratched on the shore of the river where he'd been fishing. Rage burned inside at the thought of anyone subjecting another human to the pain and humiliation of being held captive and without clothing. She had to have been desperate to make a break for it despite her lack of clothing or weapons to defend herself against a wild animal attack. She was lucky to be alive.

Reggie opened her eyes and glanced at him briefly before she began to talk in a clear, soft tone, reciting the facts of what had happened to her over the past couple of weeks.

"I was walking home from work in Bozeman, when I heard footsteps behind me. When I turned, someone flung a bag over my head and jammed a needle into my arm. I don't remember anything from that moment until when I woke up in a cool, damp cell, completely naked with only a thin blanket. I was scared and called out. I was shocked at a number of female voices answering my questions in the pitch darkness."

"You say females?" Sam frowned. "How many more of you were there?"

"Four, that I know of. Beth, Terri, Marly and Kayla." She looked up at him. "I have to get them out. No human should be subjected to what we had to endure. The man used a cattle prod to make us stay in line. Any time we protested or talked loud enough he could hear us, he used that damned cattle prod, turned up to its highest voltage." She rubbed her arm over what appeared to be burn marks, as if she'd been hit there on multiple occasions and didn't want a repeat of the pain.

"He used a cattle prod on you and the other women?" Sam said slowly, anger simmering.

She nodded. "He treated us worse than animals." Her lip curled up on one side. "If I ever get the chance, I'll kill the bastard."

The low, angry tone, filled with determination and anger, showed Reggie's strength despite what had happened.

"What can you tell me about where he held you and the others hostage?" Sam gently encouraged.

"We were kept in tiny earthen cells in what must have been the root cellar of an old house. He took us upstairs into the big house when he wanted to..." she glanced down at her hands clasped together, "hurt us."

Rage roiled in Sam's gut. For Reggie's sake, he refrained from cursing. He had to know everything in order to locate the house, the other women and the man who'd captured and incarcerated them.

"How did you get away?" he asked.

She gave a tremulous smile. "I dug my way out using the tin cup he'd given me to drink out of." Reggie stared down at her dirty fingernails. "The house was built on the side of a hill. My cell was at the end, up against the side of the hill."

"Wow." He lifted her hand and stared down at her dirty fingernails. "You must have been terrified."

She pulled her hand from his and curled her fingers into fists, more to hide the dirt than as a display of her anger at having been forcefully taken and abused. "I have to get the others out. If he thinks someone will come looking for them, he'll kill them all and hide the bodies."

Sam's back stiffened. The thought of other women like Reggie trapped and tortured, made his stomach knot and his fists clench. "We can't let that happen."

Reggie nodded. "I won't let it happen." She tossed aside the quilt and scooted her legs to the edge of the bed.

"What are you doing?" Sam asked.

"Going back."

"You're in no condition to hike up the side of a river. And you don't know how far you drifted before you washed up on shore. The river could have joined another along the way. You could have been in the water for miles."

"I can't sit around waiting for my world to align," she said. "Those women are in danger. The Master will hurt them because of me. He will take out his anger on them for letting me escape without alerting him." She snorted. "Hell, he's probably already done something to every one of them, lashing out in anger over my escape." Her eyes filled with tears. "One of the women is a young mother. She just wants to go home to her little girl." Reggie pushed to her bare feet, shivering in the cold. For a moment, she stood straight. Then her eyes rolled upward, and her face paled.

Sam reached out in time to keep her from falling to the floor. He lifted her in his arms, amazed at how light she was, even as deadweight. Gently, he laid her on the sheets and pulled the quilt over her body, tucking in the sides to keep her warm in the cool mountain air. "You need rest," he said, quietly, though she didn't hear. She'd passed out and lay as still as death.

Sam stayed at her side until she woke a couple hours later. By then, her fever had broken, and her skin was cool to the touch.

"What happened?" she asked in a gravelly voice.

"You passed out."

"I can't..." she whispered, struggling to lift her head.

"You had a high fever for quite a while. Your body burned a lot of fuel it probably didn't have to burn. You need to eat and regain your strength before you go looking for the others." He hurried to the table where Sadie had left the pot of soup. The side of the pot was still warm. He found a bowl and ladle and dished out some of the fragrant, homemade chicken noodle soup.

A moan sounded from the bed as he carried the bowl to her side. "Up to eating something?"

Reggie's eyes widened, and she inhaled deeply. "Oh, sweet Jesus, yes."

He set the bowl on the nightstand and helped her sit up, packing several pillows behind her. When he had her propped up, he gathered the bowl, dipped the spoon into the soup and raised it to her lips.

"I can feed myself—" Reggie started.

Sam slipped the spoon into her open mouth.

Her chapped lips wrapped around the spoon. Her eyelids drooped, and another moan rose from her throat.

"Are you okay?"

She nodded. "Better than okay. I don't think I've tasted anything as good." She looked up at him. "More, please?"

One spoonful at a time, he fed her the soup until he'd emptied the bowl.

By then, Reggie's eyes were half-closed, and she leaned further back against the pillows. "I'm so tired."

"You've been ill." Sam rose, place the empty bowl in the sink and returned to the bed.

By then, Reggie had rolled onto her side and slid down a pillow to lay her head on the mattress.

"Rest."

"But the others..." she whispered. "They're in danger."

"You won't be any good to them as weak as you are." Sam tucked the quilt around her and removed some of the pillows to allow her to rest her head on just one. "I'll let Hank know what you told me. He can start the hunt for the house you escaped from."

Reggie shook her head. "You can't. It will alert him that someone is looking for him. He'll kill them."

Sam touched her hand, amazed at how soft her skin was. "Hank's a smart man. He won't jeopardize their safety. He'll conduct a search on the down low."

"The Master..." She cupped her cheeks in her palms and stared at the wall. "He's smart. He targeted each of us, studying our habits, waiting until he knew no one would be watching before he made his move."

"He might have gotten away with it in the past," Sam's jaw tightened, "but we will find him and put an end to his brand of terrorism."

"Yes, please," Reggie said, her eyelids slipping downward to cover her bright green eyes.

"Rest, Reggie." Sam brushed his knuckles across her cheek, brushing a strand of her strawberry-blond hair back behind her ear. "Get your strength back. We have work to do."

CHAPTER 5

LIGHT SHONE THROUGH A GLASS WINDOW, edging past the slits of her eyelids, nudging Reggie awake. The bed was so soft, the sheets fresh and clean, and she was warm for the first time since she'd been taken. The scent of wood smoke gave her the feeling of being home, even though she knew she wasn't.

She stretched and shoved her hair out of her face, feeling how dirty it was. She needed a shower, a chance to cleanse the dirt of the past couple of weeks off her skin. Would she ever feel clean again, after what she'd endured at the hands of the Master?

When she turned onto her side, a long pink tongue snaked out and licked her cheek.

The dog Sam had called Grunt sat beside the bed, his chin on the mattress. His tongue shot out again, his entire body wagging along with his long tail. The

German Shepherd appeared to be smiling, if dogs really could smile.

Reggie reached out and scratched the dog behind the ears. When she rolled onto her back, she saw dark hair on the bed beside her.

Sam had fallen asleep with his butt in the chair beside the bed and his head on the mattress beside her hip.

She resisted the urge to touch the dark hair and feel the strands beneath her fingertips. This man had saved her life.

Grunt nudged her other hand, reminding her that he had been the one to find her. In her fevered mind, she'd thought Grunt was a wolf. As large as the German Shepherd was, he could be just as dangerous as a wolf.

Reggie smiled. The animal only wanted to be scratched behind the ear and possibly fed.

She glanced around the room illuminated dimly by the light finding its way through the windows on either side of the wooden door. There wasn't much to the room, but it had everything one would need to live comfortably, from a small kitchenette with a stove, sink and refrigerator, to a rough-hewn table and chairs, a single brown leather sofa, a small closet and a bed. Reggie assumed the door in the corner led to a bathroom. She eased out from beneath the sheets and quilt and let her legs dangle over the opposite side of the bed from Sam. She didn't want a repeat of the last time she'd attempted to get out of the bed. With Sam sleeping, he wouldn't be there to catch her if she fell.

The thought of his large, capable hands catching her made her feel warm all over and in places she hadn't expected to ever feel warm again. The thought of why made her cold all over again. The Master had used her and abused her in the worst possible ways. As he was doing to the other women held in captivity beneath his house. A shiver rippled across her skin. She felt dirty. Yes, she was dirty from running through the woods, falling into the river and lying on the muddy banks. The kind of dirty she knew wouldn't wash off was the kind that would take years to overcome. Still, she wanted a shower, more than she wanted her next meal.

When she was fairly confident she wouldn't pass out, she eased to her feet and stood for a long moment. Her head didn't spin, and she didn't wobble. Though her legs were weak, she could make it across the floor to the bathroom. Once inside, she relieved herself, washed her hands and stared into the small mirror over the sink.

Holy hell, she looked horrible! Her face was scratched and bruised, her hair lay in matted hanks with pieces of leaves and sticks twisted between the strands. She eyed the small shower for a second, checked the lock on the door and patted the fluffy white towel on the counter. The water was easy to turn on but took a few minutes to warm up. Meanwhile, she stood on the wood floor, her bare feet and legs cold from the chill mountain air.

When the water was warmer than room temperature, she stripped out of the T-shirt and hung it on a hook on the back of the door. That's when she realized she had no undergarments. She'd been naked when she'd run from the Master's place, and she hadn't cared. Her goal had been to get as far away as fast as she could. If she'd been naked when she'd left her prison, she'd been naked when Sam and Grunt had found her.

Her cheeks heated.

She couldn't do anything about the past. So, Sam had seen her naked. She hadn't been in the best condition. He must have dressed her in the T-shirt as well. And her body wasn't all that muddy from having been in the river. Had he cleaned her up before dressing her in one of his T-shirts?

Reggie's cheeks burned. With consciousness and clarity came shame and embarrassment. She lifted her chin. It didn't matter what Sam had seen and done, as long as he hadn't taken advantage of her while she'd been out of it. Her gut instinct told her he'd been a gentleman and had done only what was necessary to keep her alive and comfortable.

Reggie stepped beneath the spray and let the hot water wash away the remaining dirt and smudges she'd acquired during her race against death. She squirted shampoo into her palm and rubbed it into her hair, working up a thick lather. Then she ran the suds across her face, shoulders and breasts. Pouring more shampoo into her palm, she scrubbed lower, rubbing hard in an attempt to wash away the filth of her captor's hands and body parts. She'd never feel clean again. Not after what she'd been through. The man deserved to be shot. She prayed she'd have the pleasure of pulling the trigger. That bastard had to be stopped. Too many had already been hurt by his madness. And those Reggie knew about might not be all he had harmed.

She poured some conditioner into her palm and worked it through her hair, finger-combing the tangles free. When she'd rinsed most of it out of her hair, she turned off the water, reached for the towel and patted her skin dry. When she was done, she wrapped her hair in the towel, feeling more like the Reggie she'd been before she'd been taken. With nothing else to wear, she pulled the T-shirt back over her body, stepped out of the bathroom and ran into a solid wall of muscles.

"Oh." She stumbled back a step or two and looked up into Sam's eyes. "I thought you were asleep."

Sam gripped her elbow to steady her. "I was worried about you," he said. "You were in there a long time."

Her gaze left his and found its way to the floor

and her own bare feet. "I had to scrub all of the dirt away," she murmured.

He nodded. "I was more worried that you might have fallen. It's a good thing you came out when you did. I was about to go in after you."

Warmth filled her chest and rose up her neck into her cheeks. "It's nice to have someone worry about me. Thank you."

"My pleasure." He frowned. "I might have another clean shirt you can use."

"No need. This one will do."

He turned away and dug inside a duffel bag, pulling out a solid black T-shirt. He held it out. When she didn't make a move to take it, he shook it gently. "Seriously, you sweated in the other one when you were burning up with fever."

Her nose twitched. "When you put it that way..." She took the shirt. "Thank you. And thank you for rescuing me from the river."

Sam grunted a response and walked to the refrigerator. "What do you like for breakfast? Sadie stocked the refrigerator with eggs, bacon and soup. I make mean fried eggs, or you can have some of the soup she brought last night."

"Eggs would be good. Do you want me to make them?"

He shook his head. "I've got this. I might not know how to cook anything else, but I can cook an egg and a steak. Though my preference for the steak is to cook on a grill." He pulled a carton of eggs from the refrigerator and set it on the counter beside the small stove.

Reggie returned to the bathroom, whipped off the shirt she was wearing and replaced it with the clean black one. It smelled of men's cologne or aftershave, like Sam. She liked its woodsy scent. It reminded her of her father when he'd taken her mother out for date night.

The Master had worn a cologne. It hadn't smelled anything like this. His had had a strong, sweet scent that made her stomach churn every time he'd come near her. She'd never seen his face because he'd worn a ski mask every time he'd brought her up to the big house. But she'd recognize him by his scent.

Once she had the clean black T-shirt on, she stepped out of the bathroom. She'd like to have undergarments, but a T-shirt was more than she'd had for weeks. She wouldn't complain.

The aroma of bacon frying made her stomach rumble loudly. Reggie pressed a hand to her sunken belly. She'd lost weight while she'd been held in captivity. The Master only fed them once a day. And then it had been oatmeal or dry cereal. Protein hadn't been part of their diet. Sometimes, when he took one of them upstairs, he let them eat his table scraps, if he was in a good mood. Most of the time, he only brought them up for one thing, and if they didn't cooperate, he shocked them with either the cattle prod or a taser.

The first time he'd brought her up to the big house, he'd zip-tied her hands to keep her from fighting back. She'd waited until she was out of the basement, and then kicked him hard in the shin and ran for the front door. She hadn't gone far when she'd been struck in the back with the prongs of a taser. She'd landed face-first on the floor and lay twitching. Completely incapacitated, she'd suffered through his violation of her body. The next time he'd brought her up, he'd reminded her of what had happened the last time. Brandishing the taser, he'd led her into his bedroom and kicked the door shut behind them.

When he was kicking the door with his foot, Reggie had taken careful aim and kicked him in the balls. Then she'd kicked the taser out of his hand. Unfortunately, he'd fallen to his knees in front of the door. She'd run to the bathroom and locked herself inside. While he'd pounded on the door, she'd searched for something to cut the plastic zip-ties binding her wrists. There had been nothing sharp enough to cut through the plastic. By the time she'd realized it, the door swung open and the Master had stood holding the key up in one hand and his taser in the other.

She'd ducked, but not soon enough. The prongs

hit her in the chest, and she dropped like a sack of potatoes onto the cool tiles of the bathroom floor.

Once again, she could do nothing to defend herself. The entire time he'd raped her, she'd prayed that she would die. And if she didn't, she vowed revenge on the bastard. Somehow, she'd break free and come back to make him pay for what he'd done to her and the other women he held in his cellar.

Sam stepped in front of her, holding a plate filled with eggs, bacon and toast. "Hey. Are you all right?"

She shook free of the memories and nodded.

Sam frowned, apparently unconvinced. "Have a seat before you fall."

"I'm not that weak," she protested, but did as he suggested and sat in one of the two chairs at the little table.

He set the plate of food in front of her and went back to the stove for the other. He set it on the table and pulled two tin cups from a shelf on the wall and filled them with milk from the refrigerator.

All the while, Reggie stared at the food in front of her, salivating, waiting until Sam took the seat across from her.

"You didn't have to wait," he said. "Eat."

She grabbed the fork and dug into the eggs, shoveling them into her mouth as if this might be her last meal. After what she'd been through, she didn't take any meal for granted. Nor did she take her freedom for granted. Never again would she let a man do what the Master had done to her. She'd kill her attacker first or die trying. The problem was, she'd been tased before she could do much to defend herself. Then she'd been knocked out using some kind of drug. Even if she'd wanted to, she couldn't have fought back. The best she'd been able to do was stop eating and dig her way out of her hell.

The food she'd just eaten sat like heavy wet socks in the pit of her belly, reminding her there were other women being held just like she'd been, locked up in cold, damp cells, being raped and abused by a monster.

Sam reached across the table and covered her hand with his. "If you want to help the others, you have to be able to help yourself. You need to fuel your body to have the strength to stand up to whoever captured you and held you against your will."

She nodded and pressed a hand to her belly. "I know you're correct. But it doesn't feel right filling my face with food when the others are starving and being abused."

"They would eat, if they had the opportunity. Don't let it turn your stomach. You have to get well enough to help me find them." He gently squeezed her fingers and lifted his fork. "When we're done with breakfast, I'll call Hank and see if he's learned anything."

Her eyes filled with tears. "I wish I knew more. The Master never mentioned his name. He wore a mask, and he didn't allow us to talk or ask questions. When one of the ladies cried, he hit her with the cattle prod. We learned quickly to keep our tears and questions to ourselves." She stared down at her fork full of eggs and took the bite. Sam was right. To help the others, she had to be strong.

Soon, her plate was empty and her belly full. Setting her fork aside, she glanced up at Sam. "I'm ready to start looking."

He finished his last bite and nodded. "First, we have to get you some clothes. You can't go about town dressed like you are."

She shook her head, her brow dipping. "I can't be seen. If the Master catches wind I'm not dead…"

"We'll think of something." He took his plate and hers to the sink and ran water over them.

Reggie pushed to her feet and joined him, taking up a dishtowel. "You wash, and I'll dry."

The simple act of washing the dishes felt so normal, it made her feel guilty. It didn't take long, but this wasn't getting them to the Master's house to free the others.

Sam took the dishtowel from her and dried his hands. "I know you're anxious to get started. I was hoping to hear from Hank before we set out looking."

As if on cue, a knock sounded at the door.

Reggie's eyes widened, and her heart skipped several beats. She stepped to the side of the door and stood close to the wall, out of the way and out of immediate sight of anyone who might come inside.

"Sam?" a male voice called out. "It's me, Hank."

Sam opened the door and let his boss inside.

A blast of cool air swept into the cozy cabin along with Hank.

"Sadie sent me over with things she thought you might need." He carried an armload of clothing. He looked around the room, finally spotting Reggie. "Oh, good, you're up and getting around. Sadie will be glad to hear that."

Reggie nodded. "Please thank her for the soup and medicine."

Hank nodded. "I will. By the way, I'm Hank Patterson. And you are?"

"Reggie McDonald," she said.

"Nice to meet you." He shoved the stack of clothing toward her. "These are for you. Sadie figured you could use some clothes, seeing as you didn't have any when Sam and Grunt found you."

Reggie's cheeks heated as she took the proffered items. A rush of warmth filled her chest. "That was very nice of her to think of me."

"She was horrified to hear about what happened to you. She said to tell you that if you need anything, just ask. She'll be happy to assist." Hank smiled. "She'd have come herself, but she didn't have anyone to watch Emma for now." Hank turned to Sam. "I put Swede on searching land plats from where you discovered Reggie upstream. There's a fork in the river not far from there. He'll search both branches. It would help to know more about the topography of the land around the house where you were held captive."

Reggie shook her head. "I don't remember much. But what I do know is that the house was situated on a hill. I dug my way out of the cellar because it opened up on the side of a hill."

"Do you remember how far you ran until you came to the river?" Hank asked.

She shook her head. "All I know is that I had to get away from *him* and his Rottweilers. He had two of them."

"Did they attack you?" Sam asked.

She shook her head. "No. I got away before they could catch up to me."

Sam's eyebrows shot up. "How did you do that?"

Reggie shrugged, the moment coming back to her, making her knees shake. "The dogs were almost on me. My only two choices were to give up and go back with them or jump off a cliff." Her gaze met Sam's. "I jumped."

CHAPTER 6

SAM SHOOK HIS HEAD. Reggie had to have been terrified. He couldn't imagine what she'd gone through. No one should ever be that scared that she'd throw herself over a cliff rather than go back to what she'd come from. "You jumped off a cliff. Sweet Jesus."

"I did. Into the river below." She closed her eyes. "I hit the water hard. For a moment, I thought I'd hit rocks, it was that hard."

Hank whistled. "How high up were you?"

She opened her eyes and shook her head. "I don't know. Twenty or thirty feet? I sank all the way to the bottom." Reggie's gaze shifted to the window. "I didn't think I'd ever make it back to the surface. But I did."

"You're amazing," Sam said.

Hank stared at her. "When you hit water from

that high up, if you don't do it right, it's like hitting concrete. You're very lucky to be alive."

She nodded, wrapping her arms around herself. "The water was so cold."

"The streams up in these mountains are fed by melting snow," Hank said.

Reggie shivered. "I let the river carry me as far as it could, but my arms and legs were getting numb, and I was having a hard time keeping my head above the water. That's when the river slowed, and I was able to crawl out onto a sandy bank." She shrugged and gave Sam a crooked smile. "That's where you found me."

Sam would never forget the feeling in his gut when he'd realized the figure on the riverbank was a human.

Grunt nudged her hand.

Reggie gave the dog a soft smile. "Sorry. That's where Grunt found me."

"I can't imagine what would have happened had we not been there fishing at that time." Sam drew in a deep breath and let it out. "Grunt was barking, or I never would have gone to look."

Reggie scratched the dog's ears. "Thank you, Grunt."

Sam's jaw tightened. "He was standing between you and a gray wolf. He saved your life."

Reggie's eyes widened. "A wolf?" She lowered her head, rocking it back and forth. "I thought that was part of my nightmare." She looked up at Sam. "You mean, he was real?"

"Very real," Sam said. "I fired a shot over his head, and he ran off."

"It wasn't your day to die," Hank said.

"I was lucky to get away." Reggie hugged herself tighter. "I pray the other ladies can be saved before something worse happens to them."

"We're working on it," Hank said. "I also contacted one of my guys and his woman. She's an FBI agent."

Reggie shot a frightened glance between Sam and Hank. "No one can know I'm alive. It's crucial to let the Master think I died in the fall. I floated face-down in the river for a long time to convince the Master I was dead."

"I have them in my strictest confidence. They're going to kayak upstream from the point where Sam found you. Molly, Kujo's woman, has skills with drones. She's going to record what's on both sides of the river as they go."

"Wouldn't it be easier and faster if we hired a heli-copter pilot?" Sam asked.

Hank nodded. "And noisier. Reggie's abductor could spook and decide to get rid of the women he has locked in the basement. We have to sneak up on him. Drones are much quieter."

Reggie nodded. "Makes sense."

"In the meantime, I need the names of the other

women, so Swede can be searching the missing persons databases. If we can track where they were taken, we might discover a pattern. He might work near the places where the victims were taken."

Reggie frowned. "He had me locked up for at least two weeks. During that time, he would disappear for days at a time."

Sam's fists bunched. "With no food or water?"

Reggie snorted. "He left us with a bottle of water each."

"For days?" Hank stared at her, his face reflecting his horror.

"When he came back one time, he brought Kayla." Reggie again looked toward the window. "She was sobbing. I could hear the crackle of the cattle prod and her screams."

Hank touched her arm. "I'm sorry this happened to you and the others. We're going to do the best we can to keep you safe and rescue the other women." His eyes widened. "Wait. I forgot something Sadie sent." He hurried through the door.

Grunt followed him outside.

In a moment, Hank was back with a small box. He set it on the little table. "Sadie sent these things as well. She figured you might want to get out and about while still hiding. These are some of her props she uses when she wants to move about incognito." He lifted a dark-haired wig out of the box and held it up. "She used this the last time we were in LA together. Sadie's hot as a brunette." He smiled and dug into the box again, this time pulling out an auburn wig. "Hmm. I haven't seen her in this one. I'll bet she's hot as a redhead, too."

"Sadie is hot no matter what color her hair is." Sam grinned.

Hank grinned. "You're right. She is." He shrugged. "Anyway, there are sunglasses, hooded jackets, lipstick and wigs in this box. If you don't want anyone to recognize you, these items will help you hide in plain sight."

She gave a nod. "Good. Because I can't sit back and wait for everyone else to find the bastard. I vowed that if I was able to escape, I'd be back to help them."

"And we will help in that effort," Hank said. "First, you have to recover."

"I'm recovered," Reggie insisted.

Sam shook his head. "Less than twenty-four hours ago, you almost died."

"But I didn't." Reggie sat up straighter, as if to prove she was ready to start the journey to free the others. "The longer I wait to go back, the worse it is for them. I have to get them out. Now."

Hank nodded. "As I said, we're working finding the house. After all you've been through, do you think you could find the house? Did you see where you were going when he took you there?"

She shook her head her shoulders drooping. "But I can't give up."

"Did you see the exterior of the house in your flight to get away?"

Her entire body sagged. "No. I was in a hurry to get away. I didn't look back." She buried her face in her hands. "How will we find him, if I won't recognize the house?" Tears leaked through her fingers.

Sam's chest tightened. "We'll find them. It'll just take a little longer."

"What gets me is that he's probably from around here," Hank said.

Reggie's head jerked up, her cheeks damp, her eyes wide. "I was abducted from Bozeman. I'm not sure where the others were taken."

"That's a scary thought to think he might be someone everyone knows." Sam reached out and gathered Reggie's hand in his. "We'll find him."

Hank nodded. "Yes, we will."

"Hopefully, before it's too late," Reggie whispered.

"We'll do our best to get to him before anything happens to the others." Sam couldn't promise more. If the man got spooked by Reggie's escape, there was no telling what he would do.

"I need to get back to the ranch and check on Swede's progress. You two might want to stop by." He tipped his chin toward Sam. "I have an arsenal of weapons and gear for you to choose from, should you need it. And communications equipment, if we do a team extraction."

Sam nodded. He wanted to see Hank's setup. "If Reggie's up to it, we'll stop by later today."

"I'm up to it," Reggie quickly assured them.

Sam's lips twitched. "We'll see. You've been through a lot."

"Those ladies are still going through a lot. If I can help in any way, I want to be there. Besides, I was there. Something might trigger a memory that could be significant in our effort to find this guy."

"She's got a point," Hank said. His eyes narrowed. "But to keep him from learning that you're alive and well, you need a cover story if someone should see you riding around town with Sam."

Sam tilted his head. "I'm new in town. People don't know me. If I show up in Eagle Rock with a woman, they'll assume she's with me."

Hank grinned. "For all they know, she could be your girlfriend, fiancé or wife." He glanced at Reggie's finger. "You might be the same ring size as Sadie. I'll see what she has in her jewelry box she's willing to loan you for an engagement or wedding ring."

"Let's go with a simple gold band. Reggie can be my wife."

Reggie chewed her bottom lip. "Lies have a way of growing and becoming more complicated."

"Then we need to get our stories straight," Sam

said. "We were married two years ago in San Diego where I was stationed as a Navy SEAL."

She murmured. "I've never been to San Diego."

"It's sunny on the coast, and beautiful," Sam said.

Hank chuckled. "Don't worry, most folks around here have never been to San Diego, either."

"I can't go by my real name," Reggie said. "He knows me by Reggie. And since he followed me enough to know my habits, he might also know my last name."

"Do you have another name you can remember to respond to?"

She nodded. "My full name is Regina. My mother called me Reggie, but my high school friends called me 'Ginnie'."

Sam dipped his head. "Ginnie Franklin it is."

"Ginnie Franklin," she said, as if rolling the name on her tongue. "Married two years ago in San Diego." She turned to the pile of clothing and the wigs Hank had brought. "I'll go change, then I'll be ready for whatever we need to do." Gathering the items in her arms, she crossed to the tiny bathroom and disappeared inside, closing the door softly behind her.

Hank faced Sam. "I'm worried. We need to get moving on finding this guy ASAP. He sounds like a sociopath."

"I'm worried, too. If he does away with the other women and finds out Reggie is still alive and might be able to identify him, he'll come after her."

"Ginnie," Hank corrected. "And you're right. Ginnie is in danger, either way. He could kill her to keep her from coming back for the others, or to keep her from testifying against him." He pushed to his feet. "She'll need twenty-four-seven protection."

Sam nodded. "That's where I come in." Whether Hank assigned him to her or not, Sam had been the one to find her. He felt a sense of obligation to keep her alive. No. More than an obligation. He liked her. She'd been through hell. Instead of running away, she wanted to go back to save the others. That took a lot of courage. He admired a woman who stood up for what was right no matter the danger to herself.

"I'm headed back to see what Swede's found on the other missing women and the folks who own property along the rivers."

"We'll be there as soon as Reg-Ginnie's ready."

Hank grinned. "Congratulations on your wedding, though I'm two years late. Make sure she wears a wig. That reddish-blond hair is a dead giveaway."

Sam nodded. "We'll be sure to make her disguise a good one." He walked with Hank to the door and out onto the front porch. "And Hank, thanks for the opportunity. This might not be the assignment you had in mind for me, but assignment or not, it's the one I'll follow through to a resolution."

Hank shook Sam's hand. "That's why I hired you for the Brotherhood Protectors. We don't leave things undone." He drove away in his pickup, kicking up dust on the dirt road leading toward the highway.

Sam turned back toward the cabin to find Reggie standing in the doorway, dressed in jeans, a bulky gray sweater, black ballet slippers and the brunette wig covering her strawberry-blond hair.

Her green eyes shone brightly out of her pale face. "I'm ready to go."

"Oh, sweetheart, are you sure you can hold up?"

She squared her shoulders. "I feel much better since having something to eat. I'll make it now." Reggie lifted her chin. "Those women need me to be strong. So, I will be." Her green eyes swam in unshed tears she wouldn't let fall down her cheeks.

Sam wanted to pull her into his arms and hold her until all the bad stuff went away. But no amount of hugging would save those women. Only speed, action and determination would bring them out of captivity alive.

Reggie swayed on her feet. She straightened and pushed her shoulders back. Sam would bet she was fighting exhaustion, afraid he'd leave her behind if he thought she was too weak.

"All right then, let me grab my keys, and we'll follow Hank out to his ranch." He brushed past her, his shoulder bumping against her arm. A spark of electricity ignited in his bloodstream.

This woman had been tortured, probably raped and had nearly drowned. Top that with battling a raging fever, and she still insisted on going to the rescue of the others who were still trapped.

Sam grabbed his keys, slipped his shoulder holster over his arms and buckled it in place. Then he slid his 9 mm pistol into the holster, shrugged into his jacket and looked up to see Reggie watching his every move, her hand resting on Grunt's neck.

"You don't happen to have another one of those, do you?" She nodded toward the holster, now hidden beneath his jacket.

"Sorry. I don't. But I have a conceal carry permit. Do you?"

Reggie shook her head. "Never thought I needed to carry a gun." She snorted softly. "I guess I was wrong."

"Having a gun doesn't guarantee you'll be safe. Being fully aware of your surroundings at all times is even more important."

"I thought I was pretty aware of my surroundings." She shrugged. "I guess I wasn't aware enough."

"We can ask Hank for a weapon for you." He held the cabin door open for her. "Have you ever fired a gun?"

She passed him, her shoulder rubbing against his chest. Her eyes widened for a brief moment, and she swallowed. "My father taught me how to fire his rifle. He always wanted to take me deer hunting, but he died before I turned eleven."

"I'm sorry to hear that."

Reggie's lips twisted. "He thought he had a headache and ignored it a little too long. It turned out he had an aneurysm. He went to bed that night and never woke up. It was me and my mother against the world until she remarried after I finished high school."

"And your mother? Is she still alive?"

Reggie nodded. "As far as I know. She moved to Florida a couple years ago with her new husband. I wonder if she even knows I disappeared." Reggie shook her head. "I usually call her once a week. It's been at least two since I last talked to her. She must be beside herself, wondering why I haven't contacted her."

"We can make that call from Hank's place while we're there," Sam suggested.

"No," Reggie said. "The Master knew my name. He might be able to trace my previous calls to my mother. If I place one now, he'll know I'm not dead."

"Good point."

"I hate to leave my mother in a panic, but I can't let any more people know Reggie McDonald is alive."

"But Sam and Ginnie Franklin are alive and well and can move around without trouble." Sam snagged her arm with his hand, holding her with a light touch. "Come on, sweetheart, we'd better make this look real."

"I'd like to go back to the place where you found me."

"Will do." He held the truck door for her and helped her up into the passenger seat. She leaned on his arm as if it took a lot of effort to climb up on the running board.

He might be a fool to allow her out of the cabin so soon, but he was also convinced she'd leave without him, if he didn't let her help in the investigation. He chose to go with the flow. If she passed out, he'd lay the seat back in the truck and let her rest until she regained her strength.

With Hank and his team working on locating the house where Reggie and the other women had been held captive, Sam could concentrate on keeping Reggie alive and well. Though she would soon grow tired of him stalling her efforts.

The drive to White Oak Ranch, where Hank based the Brotherhood Protectors, took only thirty minutes. They had to pass through Eagle Rock along the way.

Reggie had slipped a pair of sunglasses over her eyes that Sadie had provided.

As a mega-movie-star, Sadie knew all the tricks of remaining incognito. Otherwise, she'd never catch a break from the paparazzi. The public was voracious in their appetite for anything to do with Sadie McClain. From what Hank had told Sam, Sadie had escaped to Montana to live a normal life with her husband and baby girl, Emma.

Reggie had an entirely different reason to remain

undercover. Her life and the lives of Beth, Kayla, Terri and Marly depended on keeping their tormentor from knowing Reggie had survived her plunge over the edge of the cliff.

At the gate to White Oak Ranch, Sam pressed the button and waited for the someone to answer.

"Sam, I didn't expect you to get here so soon," a voice said over the intercom. A camera pointed down at the cab of the truck. Hank could see the driver of the truck. "Is Ginnie with you?"

Sam nodded. "She is."

"Good. I have something I want to show the two of you."

Already, the black iron gate was sliding open.

Sam pulled through and drove along the paved road to a sprawling cedar and stone ranch house perched on a knoll, with the Crazy Mountains rising up in the background, covered in Douglas fir, Lodgepole and Ponderosa pines. The sky was a deep blue with fluffy white clouds floating over the peaks.

Before he'd left the military, Sam had never been to Montana. He hadn't been sure about the move but working with Hank had drawn him to the cold north. He'd heard the winters were brutal, but he couldn't imagine any place as wild and beautiful.

As Sam pulled up to the house, Hank stepped out onto the porch. Sadie, his wife, emerged to stand beside him, holding a little girl on her hip.

The mega-star was beautiful even without all the

Hollywood makeup and costumes. Her baby, with her soft blond curls, showed every sign of being as stunning as her mother. Hank slipped an arm around Sadie's waist and waited for Sam and Reggie to join them on the porch.

Sam hurried around the front of the truck to the passenger side.

Reggie had the door open and was sliding out of the passenger seat when he came to a stop beside her.

He waited to see if she could climb down on her own.

She placed her foot on the running board and slipped out of the seat. Her knees buckled, and she would have fallen, but her hand on the door slowed her descent.

Sam reached out and helped her the rest of the way to the ground. "Well enough, my ass," he muttered.

She shot him a narrowed glance. "I am. I just… missed my step." Reggie squared her shoulders and marched toward the porch.

Sam jerked open the back door and let Grunt out. Then he hurried to catch up with Reggie, one hand ready to grab her if she "missed her step" again.

When they neared the porch, Sam cupped her elbow and helped her up the steps.

Sadie held out her free hand. "You must be Ginnie." She winked. "Sam's told us so much about you, I feel like I know you already."

Reggie shook the proffered hand and smiled. "I can't believe I'm shaking hands with Sadie McClain."

"Sadie Patterson around here." She smiled up at her husband. "My husband made an honest woman of me."

"I don't know about honest, but if you mean I made you my wife..." Hank tightened his hold around her waist and bent to kiss her lips. "I'd say you're all right. Mmm. And you taste like sugar cookies."

Sadie laughed. "Because Emma and I just made some." She smiled at Sam and Reggie. "Come in. I have cookies fresh out of the oven. Would you like milk, lemonade, tea or coffee?"

"Coffee, if it's no trouble," Sam said.

"Milk for me," Reggie said with a crooked smile. "I like to dip my cookies."

"So do I," Sam said. "In my coffee."

Hank held open the door.

Sam turned to Grunt, "*Bleib,*" he said, giving him the German command for "stay".

The dog sat on the porch, his single eye bright and alert.

"Good boy," Sam praised the animal and followed Reggie inside.

"I'll bring the drinks and cookies down to the war room." Sadie handed Emma to Hank and strode across the massive living room to the entry into what appeared to be a kitchen beyond.

Hank tickled his daughter's belly. "Hey, you. Want to take Sam and Ginnie down the stairs to see what we've discovered?" He led the way to a door, pressed his thumb to a bio scanner and waited for the door to slide open. Stairs led down to a cool, white hallway.

Sam stood back and let Reggie follow Hank down into the basement below.

The white hallway opened out into a wide room. One wall was lined with computers, keyboards and an array of monitors.

A big man with white-blond hair sat in front of one of the arrays of monitors, clicking away on a keyboard.

"Swede," Hank said. "Meet the newest member of the Brotherhood Protectors. Sam Franklin, formerly known as Talon."

Swede glanced up and held out a hand. He didn't rise and kept his other hand on the keyboard. "Nice to meet you."

Sam crossed to the man and shook his hand. "Swede your name or nickname?"

"Axel Swenson," Swede said. "But everyone calls me Swede. Do I call you Sam or Talon?"

"I go by Sam now that I'm a civilian." Sam peered over Swede's shoulder at the monitors in front of him. Half of them were filled with images of the Montana countryside. A river ran through the middle of each screen. "Are those images of the river I was fishing on?"

Swede nodded. "Kujo and Molly are working their way upriver by kayak with a drone flying overhead." He clicked on the keyboard and four of the six monitors changed to images of women. Two were driver's license photos, two were snapshots. All were young, pretty women. One of the snapshots was of a woman with a toddler girl.

"I pulled these from missing persons reports," Swede said.

Sam leaned closer and read the names beneath the pictures. "Beth Snow. Marly Miller."

Reggie stepped up beside Sam and continued, her voice shaking, "Kayla Long and Terri Thompson." She pressed a fist to her lips, and tears spilled down her cheeks. "All missing."

"Kayla's family is offering a reward for information leading to her return," Swede said. "She's been gone a week. Marly's been missing for over a month. Beth for three weeks and Terri for about the same time." Swede ran his fingers across the keyboard again and brought up one more photo.

Reggie gasped as her driver's license photo displayed on a monitor.

"Apparently, someone turned you in as missing," Swede said.

Sam slipped an arm around her.

Reggie leaned into him, her body trembling. "Missing for two weeks," she whispered. "It felt like a lifetime."

Swede brought up a map with points illuminated. "The highlighted dots are where each of the women were taken." He touched a finger to the monitor and drew a circle around the dots. "He seems to be consistent about taking women within this area."

"That's a pretty wide area," Sam said. "It covers several counties in Montana."

Swede tapped his finger on the desk, staring at the images. "He's targeted women from Bozeman to Kalispell."

CHAPTER 7

"How does a man who goes to all these towns not get noticed?" Reggie asked. "These aren't big cities where people get lost in them."

"Research shows that predators with this level of experience are usually repeat offenders. Many have been caught before." Swede pulled up another monitor. "I've run a check on the Sexual or Violent Offender Registry and come up with a couple names we can check on." He brought up images of the men in the area who were on the registry for sexual offenses. "It would take less time if we could enlist the help of the Montana Division of Criminal Investigation."

"No." Reggie shook her head. "We can't let the Master know we're coming for him. He has to think I'm dead, and he will have no one looking for me or him."

"Do any of the people on the registry live along the rivers?" Sam asked.

"The house could be off the river a little way," Reggie said. "I ran through the woods a considerable distance before I reached the edge of the cliffs overlooking the river."

Swede nodded. "I came up with three potential suspects." He brought up the first mug shot of a man who appeared to be in his early forties. "Matthew Ogletree was convicted of raping a thirteen year old girl in Bozeman eighteen years ago. Released on parole two and a half years ago, he lives along this highway in a house owned by his parents."

Reggie squinted at the photo. "I wish I could, but I won't be able to recognize a face. He wore a ski mask every time he came to get me. Now, if you had a voice recording...I might be able to pick him out. I think he had dark eyes."

Swede clicked on a satellite image of the address and zoomed in on a small cabin.

Reggie shook her head. "The house seemed much bigger than that, and it stood on the side of a hill."

"He could have been using an abandoned house nearby," Hank suggested. "We've had a lot of wealthy people from California come to Montana to buy land and houses. They rarely come out to live in them, and only vacation in them once a year."

Reggie pinched the bridge of her nose. "I can't remember much about the place. He kept us drugged for the most part. I had to stop eating what little food he gave me to avoid the drugs he laced them with."

Sam's jaw tightened. The bastard had to die. "The sooner we find this guy, the better."

Reggie nodded. "He's pure evil. I just hope the other women are still alive."

Sam held out his hand. When Reggie placed hers in his, he held it firmly. He wouldn't let that man hurt her again. He turned to the monitors. "Who else?"

Swede brought up another image of a man with a scar stretching from the middle of his forehead to his right cheek. His eyes were brown, almost black, and his lip was curled in a snarl. "Ed Knowles spent time in prison for raping a waitress who worked in Whitefish. He lives here." Swede brought up the address on the satellite image and zoomed in. The address was a mobile home with what appeared to be abandoned vehicles strewn around the yard.

"Again, not a house and not on a hill," Reggie said. She raised her hand. "True, they could be using an out-of-state resident's house, but let's see who else you have."

Clicking on his keyboard, Swede brought up a mug shot of a man with gray eyes, bushy brows and salt-and-pepper hair. "Timothy Thomas was convicted of two counts of rape. He spent twenty-five years in prison and has been out for less than a year." Swede brought up the rapist's address on the satellite image. "He lives closest to the river in a house he owns."

Sam pointed at the house. "It's bigger than the others, and it appears to be on a hill."

"I don't know," Reggie said. "His eyes aren't as dark as the Master's."

"It could have been the lighting in the house or the ski mask that made his eyes appear darker," Hank said.

Sam watched the expressions pass over Reggie's face.

Her brow puckered, and she chewed on her bottom lip. Reggie sighed. "I wish I'd seen his face."

Sam touched he arm. "If you had, he might have killed you. He seemed pretty concerned about keeping his identity from all of you."

"I'll have Bear do a covert check on Thomas's residence," Hank said. "We can probably rule out the houses of the other two, though we can't rule out their involvement altogether. Where do these guys work? I can get some of my guys to follow them and see where they go during or after work."

"Two of them work in Eagle Rock. Ogletree works at the feed store. Knowles works at Lucky's Automotive as a mechanic. Thomas works at home as a contractor, doing graphic design work. They all report to the same parole officer in Eagle Rock."

"I don't suppose you can hack into Thomas's computer remotely?" Sam asked.

"I'm working on that," Swede assured him. "I have to get to his internet account, and through that, I can obtain his IP address. It'll take a little while."

"Good. Let us—"

"If I find anything," Swede concluded. "You'll be the first to know...after Hank, since he's been working with me in this effort."

Sam nodded and looked toward Reggie. "In the meantime, Reggie and I want to retrace our steps to the place I found her on the river."

"Just be careful," Hank warned. "If the kidnapper is concerned about finding Reggie's body, he might be out looking for her."

"Ginnie and I have our cover story, and she's rocking the wig Sadie gave her."

"We should be all right," Reggie said.

"But we'll keep a low profile to make sure no one suspects her of being the woman who got away," Sam said.

"How far up the river will you go?" Hank asked.

"As far as we can walk in an hour?" Reggie said, looking at Sam.

He nodded. "I have my pistol. Reg—Ginnie would like one as well. I can show her how to use it while we're out by the river."

Hank tilted his head toward another door. "Follow me." Sam's boss led them into another room and switched on the light. The room lit up, displaying an impressive number of weapons of all shapes and sizes, from AR-15s to .40 caliber pistols.

Reggie gasped. "I don't think I've ever seen so many weapons in one place, other than at a gun show or pawn shop."

"You've been to a gun show?" Sam asked. "And a pawn shop?"

She shook her head. "Not actually. I saw advertisements for one that was to be held at the Expo Park in Great Falls one year. Guns for as far as the eye could see. Or so it seemed. I used to go to pawn shops with my mother, looking for antique jewelry." She shrugged. "My mother liked the old pieces best."

"Is your mother still alive?" Sadie asked as she entered the room, carrying a tray loaded with cookies, milk and coffee.

"She is. She remarried and moved to Florida. They'd had enough shoveling snow to last a lifetime." Reggie chewed her bottom lip, a habit Sam noticed she did when she was worried about something. "I hope she doesn't come looking for me before we find the Master and free those women. My mother can be like a pit bull with a bone. She won't give up until she gets what she wants."

Sam fought a grin. "Much like her daughter."

Reggie nodded. "Damn right. Especially in matters of life and death. My mother won't take my death lightly."

Hank chuckled. "We'll consider ourselves forewarned." His smile faded. "Are you sure you don't want to let her know you're okay?"

She shook her head. "Too many people know I'm alive already. I can't risk it. Besides, if my mother shows up, it's one more reason for the Master to believe I'm dead."

"Fair enough. Could you hold Emma, please?" Hank handed his little girl to Sam and grabbed the tray his wife held, setting it on a counter.

Before Sam could lodge a protest, he found himself holding the child awkwardly, not sure what to do with her.

Emma had no such qualms. She smiled, giggled and planted a wet kiss on his cheek.

"She likes you," Sadie said with a smile.

Sam grinned back at Emma. "You're a little sweetheart, aren't you?" He held her closer and looked up to see Reggie staring at him.

"You look like you belong together," Reggie said. "I never thought to ask you if you were married or have children?"

He lifted one of Emma's hands. "No to both. I was never in a place, mentally or physically, to have a family. Navy SEALs belong to the Navy, twenty-four-seven. It's not a stable life for families." He shrugged. "Although some manage, others end in divorce." His gaze met Reggie's. "It's one of the reasons I left the Navy. I wanted to get on with my life."

Reggie's eyes widened. "As in having a family of your own?"

He shrugged. "Someday." He bounced Emma on his arm. "If all babies were as sweet as this one, the world would be a better place."

"I thought I wanted to have children once," Reggie murmured.

Though he wasn't staring right at Reggie, in Sam's peripheral vision, he could see her face pale and shadows darken her eyes. His heart squeezed hard in his chest. After what Reggie had gone through, he doubted she'd ever want to have sex again. Any woman who'd been raped multiple times would be rightfully wary of men. He was glad she hadn't shied away from him when he'd only wanted to help and protect her. Intuitively, he knew she needed tender care and kid gloves to get her through what was her own hell of Post-traumatic Stress Syndrome or PTSD. Finding and stopping the bastard who had done this to her and the other woman would help in her road to recovery.

He snagged a cookie for Emma and glanced at Sadie. "Can she have one?"

Sadie nodded. "Just one, though, or she won't eat her meal."

After giving Emma a cookie, Sam grabbed a glass of milk and a cookie from the tray and handed them to Reggie. "Sit and eat a cookie." He led her to a chair and urged her to sit.

"But I want a gun," she protested.

"You can choose from here. I'll bring them to you." Sam hurried toward a light, sleek .40 caliber pistol, lifted it in his free hand and felt its weight in his palm. "This one should do." He carried it to Reggie and waited while she laid her cookie and milk to the side and took the gun in her hand.

"Isn't bigger better?" she asked.

Hank chuckled. "Only if you can hold it steady." He brought her a .45 caliber pistol, a little bigger and definitely heavier. "Hold this out in front of you for thirty seconds." He took the .40 caliber from her and waited while she held the other pistol as he'd told her. After the first few seconds, her arms shook, and she nodded. "I see what you mean."

Hank handed her the .40 caliber H&K.

She held it in front of her longer than she had the other before her arms shook. "Yes, this one is better. But will it stop a man or a Rottweiler?"

"Depends on where you hit him," Sam said.

"If you hit him in the heart, it'll drop him where he stands. If you hit him in the side, he could still come at you."

"Right," Reggie said. "I need to practice."

"And we will, once we get out to the river," Sam promised. He looked to Hank. "Do you have a shoulder holster for this gun?"

Hank dug in a cabinet and pulled out what they needed, handing it to Reggie.

She slipped the straps over her shoulder.

Sam balanced Emma on one arm and adjusted the buckles with the other hand so that the straps fit snuggly against Reggie's body. His knuckles accidently brushed against the side of her breast.

Reggie sucked in a sharp breath.

"Sorry," Sam said and jerked back his hand.

"No. Really. It's okay." She gave him a hint of a smile and slid the pistol into the holster.

"Won't do you much good without ammo," Sadie noted. She handed Reggie a box of bullets.

Reggie patted the weapon, her cheeks pink. "Right. I'll take those, but I won't load until I've had a chance to familiarize myself with how to fire the gun."

"And how to use the safety switch," Sam said, his lips thinning. "Finish your milk and cookies. I'd like to get out to the river."

Reggie dipped her cookie in the milk and took a bite. Then she upended the cup and drank down all the milk. When she finished, she wiped her face with the back of her hand. She smiled at Sadie. "Thank you, Sadie. The cookies are great."

"I'm glad you liked them." Sadie wrapped four cookies in a napkin and placed them in Reggie's hands. "Here, take some extras with you. Sometimes, the guys keep working and forget we have to eat to keep up our strength."

Sam grinned at Sadie. "Hank's lucky to have you, Sadie."

"Are you kidding? I'm lucky to have him. I wouldn't be alive today, if it weren't for Hank." She took Emma from Sam. "And Emma wouldn't be here if Hank hadn't come along when he did. We're both lucky to have him in our lives." She blew a raspberry into Emma's belly. "Aren't we, sweetie?"

Emma giggled and grabbed Sadie's face, making an attempt at blowing a raspberry against her cheek. She made a loud grunting sound and slimed Sadie's cheek with spit but came up giggling.

Sadie laughed and wiped her cheek. "I'm teaching her all the wrong things."

"You're teaching her how to have fun and laugh," Hank said. "In my book, that's all the right things." He slipped a hand around her waist and pulled her and Emma into an embrace. "I'm lucky to have you both in my life."

Sam watched the display of love and devotion and envied them for what came so naturally for them. He'd known Hank when they were deployed together many years ago. He'd never seen the man as happy as he was now. It gave Sam hope for his own future.

If Hank could find happiness, so could Sam. He just had to give it time.

He turned to Reggie and studied her while she was busy adjusting the shoulder holster beneath a jacket Sadie had loaned her with the stack of clothing she'd sent earlier that day. He was amazed that she had gone from lying naked and nearly dead on the riverbank to being the cool, calm badass she appeared to be in front of him.

When he got ready to choose a woman to share his life with, he hoped he'd find someone as courageous and determined as Reggie.

Why was he even thinking in that direction? Because that was the reason he'd left active duty. He wasn't getting any younger. He'd move aside for the newer crop of Navy SEALs to take up the gauntlet, so that the life he'd put on hold while he'd served his country could begin. He wanted what Hank and Sadie had. That same level of love and companionship. And now that he'd held Emma in his arms, he had to admit, he wanted children.

Perhaps because he was so ready for this next step in his life, he was eyeing Reggie. Hell, it could be any woman he might be considering for the future Mrs. Franklin. But deep in his heart, he knew that wasn't true. He wanted someone like Reggie. He hadn't known her long, but his gut told him she was the kind of woman he needed in his life. And his gut had never steered him wrong.

Reggie wouldn't be ready or willing to embark on exploring any kind of relationship for a while. She had to work through the physical and emotional trauma of having been sexually abused. Until she'd had the time to do that, she would be strictly off limits. He wouldn't want to start something that was doomed to failure through no fault of his own.

The beauty of being out of the military was that he was on his own clock now. Nothing said he had to rush into a relationship. If someone was worth waiting for, he could wait. Not only would waiting give Reggie time to recuperate and get any help she might feel she needed, it would give him time to decide if she was really the one.

CHAPTER 8

REGGIE STUFFED the cookies into the pocket of her jacket on the opposite side of the .40 caliber pistol.

Every move she made, she could feel the cool, hard metal of the pistol against her side and the inside of her arm. Knowing she had a weapon didn't make her feel any safer than when she hadn't had one. Perhaps once she learned how to use it, she'd gain some measure of comfort. Until then, she'd just have to get used to it feeling awkward and unwieldy. Heck, maybe that feeling wouldn't get any better. Still, having something to protect herself and others was better than having nothing. She could put up with a little discomfort.

Sam tilted his head toward the stairs. "Ready?"

She nodded.

"Oh, wait," Sadie said. "I have one more item you need to add to your disguise." With her free hand, she fished in her pocket, pulling out a plain gold wedding band. She held it out to Reggie. "It's not fancy, but it's a wedding band. And if you want people to believe you two are married, you really need to wear one. It's all about what people expect to see."

Reggie frowned. "I can't take this."

"It's okay," Sadie said. "It belonged to my mother. She wasn't into wearing expensive jewelry. She was all into cooking and didn't want a big diamond to get in the way of kneading dough or washing pots and pans."

"But it's your mother's." Reggie shook her head. "I can't."

"If you don't wear a ring, people won't believe you're really married. Even if you show them a marriage certificate." Sadie placed the ring in Reggie's palm and curled her fingers around it. "I think it'll fit."

Reggie opened her hand and stared down at the simple gold band.

Sam took the ring from her and grasped her left hand. "Sadie's right. Folks will automatically assume we're married as long as they see you and me together with a wedding band on your ring finger." He slipped the ring on her finger and smiled. "I do so solemnly swear to be the best pretend husband you could ever have and to protect you from harm to the best of my ability."

Her pulse quickened, and her body flushed with

heat at Sam's softly spoken words. "And I promise to be your best pretend wife…oh, and not to forget your name."

He grinned and brought her hand up to press a kiss to the backs of her knuckles. "There. Married, and it was pretty painless, if you ask me." He winked.

Reggie smiled, though her smile faded at the thought of what they'd have to overcome to really be married. Or rather, what she'd have to overcome. Having been raped several times by the Master, she wasn't sure she could ever enjoy sex again. She never wanted to be in the position of being trapped beneath a man, forcing himself on her. A shiver rippled down her spine at the images seared into her memory.

Sam brushed a strand of her hair back behind her ear. "It's okay. I won't let anyone hurt you," he whispered.

How did he know what she'd been thinking? She looked up into Sam's eyes. In her gut, she knew he would never be the kind of man to force himself on a woman. He'd been a gentleman the entire time he'd been taking care of her. He'd handled her with care and concern. Sam was the kind of man who, if they weren't in such dire circumstances, could make her want to date him and eventually let him touch her intimately. "Thank you," she responded, turned and led the way out of the basement and through the massive living room to the front door. Grunt lay on the porch in the sun. When they came out, he sat up, stretched and trotted over to stand beside Sam.

Once outside, Reggie drew in a deep breath and let it out along with some of the tension she hadn't known was tightening her shoulders while they'd been in the Brotherhood Protectors war room basement.

She drew in another deep breath as if she couldn't get enough.

Sam touched a hand to the small of her back. "Are you okay?"

She nodded. "I don't think I'll ever like being in a basement again, no matter how nice it is, or how well-lit. It's still in the ground."

"And makes you feel trapped." Sam nodded. "I'll try to remember that and avoid taking you down there in the future."

She shook her head. "Don't worry about me. We needed to see what Swede had found. And what he showed us gives us a starting point, which is more than we had before arriving here."

Sam opened the passenger door of his truck and held it for Reggie. "Hopefully, Kujo and Molly will have some luck exploring the river with the drone."

"Meanwhile, I'd like to do some of my own exploring on foot," Reggie said as she climbed into the seat.

"Not too far," Sam said with a frown. "Remember,

you fought a fever last night. You don't want to end up having a relapse."

"I'm feeling better every minute." She patted the cookies in her pocket. "And I have extra sugar to fuel me for a while."

Sam rounded the hood of the pickup and held open the back door open for Grunt. The German Shepherd leaped up into the back seat.

After closing the door, Sam settled behind the steering wheel.

As they drove toward town, Reggie viewed the countryside. "I've lived in Bozeman most of my life, and I've been to Yellowstone, the Tetons and Glacier National Park, but I can't recall ever driving out near Eagle Rock."

Sam tilted his head toward the hills basking in the midday sun, the peaks still coated in patches of snow. "Hank tells me those are the Crazy Mountains. He grew up near here."

"But you didn't?" Reggie asked.

"No. I grew up in California close to San Diego."

"How does a San Diego boy come to live in the cold north?" She gave him a crooked grin. "You do realize it gets down well below zero during the winter, don't you?"

"I've heard," he said, a smile quirking at the corner of his lip. He slowed to take a tight curve. "I've been in cold climates before."

Reggie snorted. "Cold, yes. But have you been in

minus 45 degrees with a windchill factor of minus 65?"

"Not quite. But I'm sure I can handle it."

"Not many people who've always lived in the warm southern climates last long up here," Reggie warned.

He chuckled. "Don't worry. I'm not easily scared away by a little weather."

She crossed her arms over her chest and stared forward, nodding her head, a smirk pulling at her lip. "Yeah. We'll see."

"I came here because of the job. But more because of the Brotherhood."

Reggie turned to stare at him. "You and Hank mentioned the Brotherhood Protectors. What is that?"

"Hank was medically retired from the Navy SEALs and came back to his home in Montana because his father needed help on his ranch. He reunited with his high-school sweetheart."

"Sadie McClain is his high school sweetheart?" Reggie shook her head. "Wow. That's an interesting fact."

"Hank said Sadie was being stalked and terrorized. Someone was trying to kill her. Hank stuck to her like glue and soon figured out Sadie's sister-in-law was jealous of Sadie and was trying to kill her."

"Wow. I didn't know that. How come I didn't see that in the news?"

"Hank and Sadie wanted to spare her brother. He wasn't involved. The ex-spouse is now in jail." Sam continued, "Anyway, Hank realized Montana had become a mecca escape for rich folks. And rich folks come with their own baggage and the need for protection. He started the Brotherhood Protectors to provide a security service for people who need help and don't know who to turn to."

"Like me."

He nodded. "Like you."

"Where does he get people he can trust to do the job and not be corrupted?" Reggie asked.

"He mans it with men who've been highly trained in weapons and combat skills. Men who are good at thinking on their feet and would do anything to protect those they are responsible for. He hires former special operations men from the Navy SEALs, Delta Force, Marines and Rangers."

"Men with some serious skills in combat and self-defense," Reggie said. "Wow. I'm impressed."

"Not only does he have skilled men, he gives these skilled men a place to work, using the skills they've trained so hard to acquire. Some leave the military like Hank having been medically retired. Others, like me, are looking to start living outside a war zone."

As they neared Eagle Rock, Reggie pulled the visor down and checked her disguise in the mirror. She adjusted the dark wig and settled the sunglasses over her eyes.

"Don't worry," Sam said. "You don't look anything like the woman I found on the riverbank."

"Good." She studied the houses and streets as they passed several buildings. One had a sign hanging in front of it proclaiming it the Blue Moose Tavern. Further along was a building marked Sheriff's Department. As they left town, they passed an elementary school with cars parked out front.

"It's a cute little town," Reggie remarked. "Hard to think a serial rapist lives here or nearby. And none of the women he's holding captive came from here."

"Sounds like he doesn't want to target women too close to where he lives," Sam said.

They headed out on a highway leading west of town and soon turned off onto a narrower paved road. A few miles farther, Sam turned left onto a dirt road that became increasingly bumpy as they went.

"I don't remember anything about you bringing me out of here," Reggie said.

"That's because you were out cold in the back-seat." He shot a glance her way. "When I found you, I wasn't sure you were alive. If I'd been a few minutes later and Grunt hadn't been there…" He faced forward, his jaw set in a grim line. "The outcome would have been significantly different."

Reggie nodded. She would have been dead. Beth, Marly, Terri and Kayla would have had no one out here trying to find and free them from that monster.

Sam finally pulled to a halt in a grassy area that sloped downward to the river.

For a moment, Reggie sat staring at the water, mesmerized by how smooth and peaceful it seemed. The last time she'd been in that river, she had been fighting to stay alive, first by escaping a madman, and then his dogs. Then she'd struggled to keep her head above water in the frigid snow melt that came from the mountains.

"We don't have to do this," Sam said quietly beside her.

For a moment, she debated telling him to turn around and go back to the little cabin where he'd taken her to recuperate. But she couldn't hide. Lives depended on her.

Reggie squared her shoulders. "No. I'm okay."

Sam dropped down from the truck and hurried around to open her door and the back door to the pickup. Grunt leaped out and ran off.

Reggie frowned as she accepted Sam's hand and let him help her down onto the uneven ground. "Will he get lost?"

"So far, he's come back every time."

"How long have you had Grunt?"

Sam snorted. "A week. I adopted him after he'd been retired from military service. His handler was killed on our last mission. Grunt was injured, he lost an eye, and he spooks too easily over loud sounds since he was caught in an explosion. Because he'd become too skittish for a war zone, they put him up for adoption. Fortunately, I'd already let them know I wanted him. He deserves a forever home with someone he knows and who knows him."

"Were you and his handler close?" Reggie asked.

"As close as you get when you're deployed together. Sgt. Bledsoe and Grunt saved our asses on more than one occasion, locating explosives before we walked over them. Unfortunately, a Taliban rebel tossed a shrapnel grenade in front of them in a narrow alley. They didn't have a chance to dodge it or get away."

The tightness in Sam's voice made Reggie's chest constrict. She'd been through a hell of one kind, but Sam had been through the hell of war. She reached out and touched his arm. She couldn't think of any words that could take away the pain of losing someone you cared about, so she stood for a moment in silence.

Grunt broke the silence by loping into view and coming to a skidding halt in front of them, his tongue lolling, the damaged eye appearing like more of a wink than a battle scar.

Reggie laughed. "I believe Grunt has the hang of being a civilian already."

"I'd never seen an animal happier to see me than Grunt when I picked him up at Lackland Air Force Base in Texas. He's even a good traveler."

"You drove all the way from Texas to Montana?"

Sam nodded. "We did." He scratched behind Grunt's ear. "He's relaxed a lot, but he's still a highly trained animal. We just don't have a lot of need for his skills sniffing bombs. But he does come in handy for finding and protecting damsels in distress."

Reggie reached out and patted the dog's head. "He is an amazing animal."

Sam took Reggie's hand. "The bank is a little steep and can be slippery if it's wet."

She didn't pull her hand free, preferring the help when her knees were still a little weak. She'd never admit it to Sam, though.

He led her to the bank where a fishing pole lay in the grass. Sam bent to retrieve the pole, shaking his head. "I'm surprised this is still here."

"I'm sorry I ruined your fishing trip," Reggie said. "That gear has to be expensive."

"You didn't ruin my fishing trip. You made it..." he smiled, "more interesting."

Reggie snorted. "Interesting is the word you use when you don't want to insult the person you're talking about by saying *it sucked.*"

"No, really," Sam said. "I've never been fly fishing. A lot of my buddies told me how great it was, and that I should do it since I was going to Montana." He shrugged. "I had a week to kill before I officially started work. So, I bought the gear and did what people do when they come to Montana. I tried my hand at fly fishing." He raised his eyebrows. "I think I like the old cane pole and worm kind of fishing better."

"You had a week to kill before starting to work for the Brotherhood Protectors?" Reggie frowned. "So, you didn't get your week of vacation. I'm so sorry. You were active duty and a Navy SEAL. I'm sure you needed it."

Sam shoved a hand through his hair. "Actually, I wasn't sure what to do with it. I've spent most of the past eleven years surrounded by people. It kind of scared the shit out of me going on a vacation by myself." He smiled. "So, you see, you saved me from a fate worse than death...being alone on my vacation."

Her heart swelled at his kindness. He was a balm to her ravaged soul. Just what she'd needed after what she'd endured. "You had Grunt," she pointed out.

"You might not have noticed," Sam nodded toward the dog, sniffing at a frog, "but he's not much of a conversationalist."

The frog leaped. Grunt jumped back.

Reggie laughed. "He might not talk much, but he's good entertainment. And I'm sure he's happy you saved him from life in a kennel."

Sam's smile faded as he looked at Grunt chasing after the frog. "There were so many more awaiting adoption. I'm thinking Grunt needs a friend."

Reggie watched Sam, glad he was the one to find her and sad at the same time. If only they'd met under different circumstances. She still felt dirty and violated and wasn't sure when that feeling would fade or ever go away.

She squared her shoulders. "Okay, Grunt, time to go to work. Where did you find me?"

Grunt looked up at his name and tilted his head to one side, his bad eye winking at her. He took off downstream.

"Is that the way he found me?"

Sam chuckled. "He's not much of a conversationalist, and he can't understand all human words. No. He's headed downstream. We found you upstream." He cupped her elbow gently.

Reggie didn't even flinch when he did. Because she was still a little on the weak side, she appreciated his assistance moving along the uneven ground, working their way upstream.

When they came to a grassy area and a small sandbar jutting out into the river, Sam stopped.

Reggie gulped, swallowing a lump forming in her throat. "Here?" She looked up to Sam.

He nodded. "You were lying face-down in the sand. I thought you were dead."

Reggie's gaze followed the footsteps to an imprint in the sand where her body must have been. She knelt and touched the cool sand, her eyes filling. "Thank you," she said.

Grunt loped up to stand beside her, his gaze on the brush on the other side of the sandbar.

"What's wrong, Grunt?" Reggie stared in the same direction as the dog but didn't see anything in the shadows of the bushes. "What's he growling about?" She turned toward Sam.

Sam had his hand in his jacket, reaching for his gun. He pulled it out, his mouth set in a grim line. "He had a stand-off with a wolf the last time we were here."

As quickly as he'd started growling, the dog stopped and bumped her playfully with his wet nose. He ran over to the brush and sniffed around before he hiked a leg and peed on the lower branches.

Reggie laughed. "I guess he's marking his territory in case the wolf comes back."

Sam nodded, his shoulders relaxing as Grunt ran back to where they stood. The dog appeared relaxed, as if no danger existed in the immediate vicinity.

Reggie straightened and walked along the river's edge, heading further upstream. The more she walked, the more her gut tightened.

"Kujo and Molly have to be quite a way up the river by now." Sam looked into the distance where the river curved to the north. "We'd be better off going back to Hank's and reviewing the video from the drone."

"I know it's crazy to think we could walk all the way back to the cliff where I jumped. It could be miles away," Reggie said, continuing to walk along the bank, not ready to turn back and admit defeat.

"The river was moving much faster there. Not like it is here. I'd call this meandering, barely flowing. Where I jumped in, it was deep, and the water swept me away."

Grunt ran ahead, plowing into the water as if he saw something moving beneath the surface and running back out to shake away the water from his coat.

As Sam kept pace with Reggie, he slipped his hand from her elbow to capture her fingers with his. She liked the way his big hand held hers firmly so that she wouldn't fall. Yet, she knew if she wanted to let go, he wouldn't hold on. He'd release her. Knowing she had the choice made her want to keep holding his hand.

The terrain grew steeper and rockier. Reggie climbed up a hill that overlooked the river below. The hill sloped back down on the other side and rose again to an even higher hill covered in Lodgepole pines and other evergreens. She didn't see any actual cliffs in the distance, but then the river curved back behind the next hill, and there weren't any houses close to the river. At least, none that she could see.

She sighed. "I don't know what I expected to find, but it's not here where I can see it." She turned to face Sam. "I guess we'd better head back before it starts getting dark."

Gunfire ricocheted off the hills.

"Get down!" Sam jerked Reggie's arm, hauling her down to the ground.

Something crashed through the trees and underbrush, running in their direction.

Grunt shot off in the direction of the noise, his usual barking silent.

"Grunt!" Sam called out.

The dog didn't slow or stop, disappearing into the underbrush.

Another shot rang out, and the crashing ceased.

Reggie froze close to the ground, her heart pounding.

CHAPTER 9

Sam had his gun out, his gaze glued to the direction Grunt had gone. He prayed the last gunshot hadn't been aimed at the retired military war dog. If Grunt was dead, Sam would kill the bastard who'd shot him.

Who would be firing off rounds during this time of year? It wasn't hunting season. Whoever had been shooting couldn't be target practicing with only two shots, unless the gun had jammed. The only other reason Sam could think someone would be shooting was at them. He hated leaving Reggie, but he had to find out who was doing the shooting and at what. If it was someone shooting at them, he'd take him out. And he couldn't do that with Reggie at his side.

He glanced around and found a large boulder near to where they were crouched below the top of the hill. "See that boulder?" he whispered.

Reggie's gaze darted to where he was pointing, and she nodded, her eyes wide, her face pale.

"We're going to crawl to that boulder and get behind it."

Reggie made no move toward the boulder. She remained frozen in place.

"Come on, Reggie. I'll go with you. But you have to move." He took her hand. "On three. One…Two… Three." He started toward the boulder, tugging on her hand.

Eventually, she moved, crawling on her hands and knees until she rounded the boulder and hunkered behind it.

Sam waited for a moment and tipped her chin up to face him. "Are you okay?"

She nodded.

"Let me hear you tell me you're okay."

She swallowed hard and whispered. "I'm okay."

"Good. I want you to stay here. Don't move. Don't make a sound. I'm going after whoever fired those shots."

Reggie's hand shot out, grabbing his arm. "No. Don't leave me."

He patted her hand and disengaged it from his arm. "We can't stay here and hide forever. It'll get dark and make it dangerous for us to walk back along the river."

"What if he was shooting at us? What if he shoots

you?" She turned her hand and gripped his. "I don't want you to die."

"Reggie, this is what I do. I'm trained for this kind of mission. I'll be all right." He brushed his lips across her forehead. "Trust me."

"Promise me you won't die," she said, her gaze on his, a frown marring her brow.

He held up his hand as if swearing in court. "I promise. Now, let me go before he finds us or gets away. And I need to check on Grunt."

Her frown deepened. "Do you think he shot Grunt?"

"I won't know until I go look." He uncurled her fingers from his jacket sleeve and gave her a pointed look. "Stay down and keep quiet. I'll be back as quickly as I can."

He left her hunkered low behind the boulder and eased his way through the brush in the direction Grunt had gone. The dog had a good nose for finding more than bombs. If anyone could find the shooter, it was Grunt. Sam prayed the last shot hadn't been at the dog.

Sam moved through the trees and underbrush, keeping to the shadows, his gun drawn.

Rustling in the leaves made him stop and listen.

Grunt's bark made him start moving again. If the dog was barking, he hadn't been injured. Sam reasoned that Grunt would whine if he'd been hit.

He followed the sound of Grunt's barking and

came to a small forest glen between tall pines.

Grunt stood near the center, barking at something lying on the ground.

The figure on the ground kicked four long, slender legs.

From what Sam could see, they were the legs of another animal. It was too small to be an elk. It had to be a deer.

Sam sensed more than saw movement at the other side of the clearing. A teenaged boy stood near the edge of the glade, a rifle raised to his shoulder, aiming at Grunt.

Sam's heart skipped several beats. "Don't shoot!" he shouted and ducked low.

The boy swung his weapon toward the sound of Sam's voice and fired off a round.

The bullet went wide, missing Sam completely.

The boy's eyes widened, and he muttered a curse and took off running away from the glen, the deer and Sam.

Sam holstered his gun and ran after him. Grunt ran ahead.

"Grunt, *bleib*!" Sam yelled, afraid the dog would get caught up in the chase and rip into the boy.

Grunt skidded to a halt and remained where he stood as Sam ran past.

It took him far too long to catch up to the teen. Only by anticipating his moves did Sam finally catch him in a flying tackle.

The boy slammed to the ground, his rifle skittering out of his reach in the dust.

"Let me go!" the teen grunted, pinned to the ground beneath Sam's heavier body.

"Not until you tell me what the hell you were doing?" Sam sat up, yanked one of the boy's hands behind his back and up between his shoulder blades.

"Hey, not so hard," the young man said. "That hurts."

"Yeah. And being shot at can get a man killed." Sam gripped the teen's elbow and yanked him to his feet. "Explain yourself."

The teen dipped his head, refusing to look Sam in the eye. "I don't have to explain anything. I got just as much right to be out in the woods as anyone else. It's a national forest, which makes it public property. Now, let go of me." He jerked his arm but couldn't free it from Sam's grip.

"You might have a right to be in the woods, but it isn't hunting season. Let's go back to that clearing and see what you've been up to."

"I don't know what you're talking about."

"Maybe going back there will remind you." Sam started for the clearing.

"I can't leave my rifle. It's all I have."

Sam reached down and grabbed the rifle in one hand without letting go of the teen. Then he marched the young man back to the clearing where the animal lay on the ground near Grunt.

It was a white-tail deer, shot through the chest, no longer kicking. It lay still. Dead.

"Care to explain where that wound came from?" Sam used the rifle to point at the bullet hole.

"It was an accident," the boy said. "I was doing some target practice when that deer ran out in front of my bullet."

"Yeah, and I'm George Washington."

"You're George, and I'm Abe. So, let go of me." He leaned away from Sam, his feet digging into the ground.

"Why are you hunting out of season?" Sam demanded. "You might as well tell me. I'm not letting you go until I get some answers."

The teen twisted and turned but couldn't break free of Sam's stronger grip. Finally, he stood still, his shoulders slumped, a scowl on his young face. "Hunting season is dumb."

"Why?"

"A person's gotta eat more than just in the fall during hunting season. What's he supposed to do the rest of the year?" He kicked his worn boot across the ground.

Sam stared closely at the young man. He was painfully thin, and his clothes were torn and threadbare. The oversized jacket he wore hung on bony shoulders with holes in the elbows. His boot laces were only tied halfway up as if the laces had been broken off too many times to go any higher.

"You're hunting for food?" Sam asked, his voice less stern, concern replacing anger.

"What do you think I'm doing? A guy's gotta eat." He tipped his chin toward the deer. "That'll feed us... me for a week." He glared up at Sam. "You got your answers. Now, let go of me."

Sam's eyes narrowed. "If you were hunting for food, why were you aiming at my dog?"

"I shot that deer fair and square." The boy's chin lifted, defiantly. "I wasn't going to let no stray dog eat it before I got the chance."

"What's your name?" Sam demanded.

"I told you," he said. "You're George, and I'm Abe."

"Where do you live?" Sam asked.

"I ain't gotta tell you nothin'," Abe said.

"Okay, then, you're coming with me." Sam led him back the way they'd come, collecting Grunt along the way to the boulder where Reggie hid. "Ginnie, you can come out. I've caught the shooter."

Reggie peeked out from behind the rock, her brow forming a V. "That's a kid."

"I know. And he was shooting this." He held up the rifle. "Since he refuses to take me to his home, we're going to take him back to Eagle Rock and turn him over to the sheriff."

Abe fought to get away. "You can't take me to the sheriff. I gotta go home."

"Not if you don't take me with you," Sam said. "Those are your choices. You take me to your home,

122

or I take you to the sheriff and let *him* take you home or to jail. It'll be up to him."

The teen glared at Sam for a long moment.

"Guess we're going to the sheriff." Sam pushed the boy toward the trail leading back the way he and Reggie had come.

"Okay, okay, I'll take you to my house," Abe said, a frown denting his forehead. "But can we take the deer with us?"

"Isn't that a little heavy for someone your size to carry through the woods?" Sam asked.

The boy again lifted his chin. "I can carry twice my weight as long as it's strapped to my back. Besides, it was a little deer."

Sam kept his grip on the teen all the way back to where the deer lay on the ground.

"You gotta let me go long enough to field dress it," the boy said. "I'm not carrying the whole thing back, just what's edible."

Sam couldn't believe he was going to let the young man loose to field dress the deer, but he suspected the deer was all the kid had to eat. So, he helped him dress the deer and strap what was usable to the boy's back.

"We gotta hurry. When it gets dark, the wolves come out. They'll take what's mine, if I let 'em." Abe led the way down the hill, picking his way across a ravine and through tall stands of pines and Douglas firs.

As they came to another clearing, Abe stopped and turned to Sam, his brow furrowing. "Look. You can take me to the sheriff, or whatever, just don't do it until Mama gets home to watch out for the young'uns." He glanced down at Grunt. "Does your dog bite?"

"No," Sam said.

"Well, keep him close. I don't want him causin' trouble." Abe descended a hillside into what was little more than an old deer camp, complete with shoddy camp trailers arranged in a semicircle around a native stone fire pit.

He stopped by the stone circle and let the deer carcass slide off his narrow shoulders onto the stones. "You all gonna stand there starin' or come help me get this meat cut up and ready to cook?"

Sam glanced around at what had, at first, appeared to be a deserted camp.

Then, one by one, children emerged from the shadows of the trailers and the brush surrounding the camp.

"They're just babies," Reggie whispered beside him.

Sam's gut clenched as he counted. One...two...three, four...five. The fifth was a female of maybe thirteen or fourteen, carrying a baby that couldn't have been more than six months old. All of them wore ragged clothing and needed a bath.

The teenaged girl handed the baby off to another

girl a couple years younger and hurried forward. "Abe, what you doin' bringing strangers home with you? You know Mama doesn't like us talkin' to strangers."

Sam's lips twitched. So, the boy hadn't been lying when he'd said his name was Abe. "Who are all these children?" Sam asked.

Abe stood with his feet slightly apart, his shoulders back and his head held high. "These children are my family. Ain't no one gonna split us up or send us off in different directions. Our mama is takin' care of us. We don't need no stinkin' government ladies shipping us off to foster homes."

Sam held up his hands. "I'm not with the government. But is it safe for you all to be out here alone without adult supervision?"

"Mama's our adult supervision." The teenaged girl came to stand beside Abe. "We don't need anyone else."

"Where's your father?" Reggie asked.

Abe spit on the ground. "The bastard ran off after baby Jake was born. Damned drunk and coward. Beat up on Mama every chance he'd get."

The girl's lip curled back in a snarl. "We're better off without him. One less mouth to feed." She tipped her chin toward Sam and Reggie. "What do you want with us?"

Sam scratched his head. "I wanted to make sure Abe got home with his kill."

"Well, I'm home," Abe said. "You can leave now."

"I'd like to talk to your mother before we go."

Abe shot a glance at his sister. "She don't get home for a while. She works late at the tavern."

The teenaged girl nodded. "She'll pitch a fit if she knows we been talkin' to strangers."

"Well, I'm Sam, and this is Ginnie." He turned to Reggie and back to Abe. "You know our names, so now we're not strangers."

"Not falling for that load of bullshit." Abe crossed his arms over his chest. "You gonna turn me over to the sheriff?"

Sam shook his head. "No, but you can't be hunting out of season. Someone else might catch you who won't be willing to look the other way."

"Like I said, hunting season is dumb. We gotta eat all year long, not just in the fall." His gaze swept the faces of the little kids gathered around them, their eyes wide.

A tiny girl tugged on Sam's jacket. "Are you gonna take Abe to the sheriff?"

"No, ma'am." Sam squatted next to her and looked her square her bright blue eyes. "I just don't want him to get into trouble."

"The only trouble I'll get into is if you say anything to anyone about me and my family." Abe met Sam's gaze, his own intense.

Sam suspected the boy, as the oldest, was in charge nearly twenty-four-seven. He couldn't show any sign of weakness, or the others would have no one to guide them and keep them safe.

"I won't do anything to harm you or your family." He didn't like it, but he and Reggie had to get back to the truck before the sun dipped below the ridge line. "We'll be going back the way we came."

"Do you know how to get back?"

"I'm pretty sure," Sam said, although the teen had taken them through the woods at a pretty quick pace.

Abe shook his head. He turned to the girl. "Lizzy, you and Josh cut up the deer and put some in a pot to boil. I'll be back before dark." He turned back to Sam and Reggie. "Let's go."

"You don't have to lead us back," Sam said. "You need to stay here."

"Lizzy can handle things while I get you back to where you came from." He took off toward the woods and stopped at the edge of the clearing to turn back. "You comin' or not?"

Sam grinned. "Coming." He took Reggie's hand and hurried her toward the teen. Grunt fell in step beside them.

As they walked through the woods, Sam asked, "You know these hills pretty good?"

Abe nodded without slowing his pace. "Lived here all my life."

Which couldn't be more than fourteen or fifteen years. Not much, but enough for a young man with a need to feed his family to find his way around the backwoods.

"Do you know of a place along the river where there are cliffs about twenty or thirty feet high?"

Abe glanced over his shoulder, still moving forward. "Yeah. But it's not on this branch of the river.

"What do you mean?" Sam asked.

"The river splits about a mile or two upstream and comes back together not far from here," Abe said.

"Which branch are the cliffs on?" Reggie asked.

"The north branch." Abe slowed and glanced back at Reggie. "Why do you want to know?"

"I heard it was really pretty and a place I should see," Sam said.

Abe came to a full stop. "Look, Sam or George, or whoever you are. We might be poor, but we're not stupid. What business do you have at the cliffs?"

Reggie's gaze caught Sam's.

Sam faced the boy. "Abe, some things are best left unsaid for good reason. For your protection, as well as ours. Kind of like not telling the sheriff about your hunting out of season."

Abe's eyes narrowed briefly. Then he nodded and continued through the woods until they came to the boulder where Reggie had been hiding. "I got you back here. You're on your own now."

Abe turned back the direction they'd come.

"Abe," Sam called out.

The teen stopped and looked over his shoulder, a frown on his brow.

"You're a good man, Abe." Somehow, someway, he had to help Abe and his family. But it would have to be after they found the house with the women. He dug his wallet out of his back pocket and extracted a one-hundred-dollar bill and one of the business cards Hank had made up for him. "Call me, if you and the kids run into any trouble. We have something to take care of, but we'll be back to check on you. So, maybe don't shoot before you check to see who it is."

When Sam held out the money, Abe's eyes widened, and he shook his head. "No, sir. I can't take that. We don't take charity."

"Abe, you worked for it. You gave us information we needed to know and led us back through the woods so that we wouldn't get lost." Sam took Abe's hand, laid the bill in it, along with the business card, and curled the boy's fingers around them. "You earned it. And keep the card in case you need anything."

The teen looked up at Sam. "Thank you, sir." Then he spun and ran down the hill, disappearing into the forest.

Sam gripped Reggie's elbow and led her along the trail paralleling the river.

"You think Abe and his family will be okay?" Reggie asked.

"They have to be. At least until we can find that house and free those women."

"We're coming back then, aren't we?" she asked. "I can't stand the thought of all those babies living the way they do. Their mother must be beside herself."

"If they even have one," Sam said through gritted teeth.

Reggie glanced his way, her eyes rounding. "You think he was lying about her working at the tavern? You think those kids are out there all alone?"

"I don't know what to think. But I don't like any scenario I can come up with." He kept moving. They had to get to the truck and contact Hank to let him know the cliff was on the northern branch of the river. If Kujo and Molly had taken the southern branch, they would have missed the cliffs. They'd have come close, but not close enough.

With the sun slipping low on the hilltops, they needed to get back to Hank's place and put the pieces they'd gathered together with whatever Hank's team had come up with in their investigation of the men from the Sexual and Violent Offenders Register and the county land records. Perhaps, that would help them narrow down the location of the house close to the cliff where Reggie had made her leap into the river.

CHAPTER 10

REGGIE FORCED herself to focus on the plight of the women being held prisoner in the Master's basement. She couldn't let herself be sidetracked by a group of children trying to make it on their own in the hills of the Crazy Mountains. Time might be running out for Beth, Kayla, Terri and Marly, whereas Abe had a handle on his siblings, for the time being. They had the deer to feed them for a week.

Already, a night had passed, and another full day, since Reggie's escape. Her mind played all the scenarios the Master could have enacted against those poor women.

By the time they reached the truck, her body was running on fumes. She was weak, and her knees shook so badly, she couldn't climb up on the running board.

Sam must have noticed, because he scooped her up in his arms and deposited her in the passenger seat without saying a word. He hurried around the other side of the truck, held the door for Grunt, and then climbed into the driver's seat. Soon, they were on their way back down the dirt road to the highway. The sun had sunk below the ridgeline, casting the road and hills into dark gray shadows.

So deep was she in her own thoughts about the women, the children and the Master, that they arrived in Eagle Rock before she realized they'd traveled that far. As they passed the Blue Moon Tavern, her hand shot out, as if of its own accord to touch Sam's arm.

He slowed immediately and pulled into a parking place beneath the wooden sign. "Are you thinking the same thing I am?"

She nodded. "You know we forgot to ask Abe what his mother's name was."

"That thought had crossed my mind, too." Sam shifted into park and got out. He snapped a lead on Grunt's collar and tied the line to streetlight pole, giving the dog just enough room to move around and lie down. "Stay," he commanded.

"Will he be okay out here by himself?"

"Yeah. I'd leave him in the truck, but he could stand some fresh air while we eat. I don't know about you, but I'm hungry, and we need to fuel our bodies for what comes next. Whatever that might be."

Reggie didn't argue. She didn't like being weak and knew a lot of her weakness was due to malnutrition for the past couple of weeks, as well as inactivity, due to being locked in a cell in the dark.

"Come on, Ginnie," he winked. "We need to eat and ask questions."

"As long as we don't out the kids to the authorities," she reminded him quietly. "We promised."

"I know what we promised." Sam's mouth drew downward into a frown. "I'm not too happy about that promise, but I understand why they don't want the government involved. With so many siblings, the only option would be to split them up into a number of foster homes."

Reggie nodded. "Abe has too much responsibility on his young shoulders."

"One crisis at a time," Sam said. "But we can at least solve one mystery while we're eating. Which we have to do anyway." He took her hand and led her into the tavern where they waited to be seated.

A pretty young brunette led them to their table. While they sat, the young lady gave them menus and told them about the night's specials. "If you have any questions, your server will be able to answer them." With a smile, she left Sam and Reggie to peruse the list of items offered at the tavern.

A waitress came to an abrupt halt beside their table and pulled a pencil from behind her ear and pad from her apron. "Hi, I'm Maggie, I'll be your waitress this evening. What can I get you to drink?"

"Feels wrong to not order a beer, but could you bring me a cup of coffee? Black?" Sam asked.

Maggie grinned. "I can do that." She turned to Reggie. "And you?"

After being held captive in the basement of a madman's house, sitting in a tavern with a perky young woman smiling at her and asking her what she'd like to drink suddenly seemed so surreal, it overwhelmed Reggie. "I'm sorry." She pushed back from the table and made a dash in the direction of what she hoped was the bathroom.

Behind her, she heard Maggie say, "Was it something I said?"

Reggie didn't care, she had to get away before she had a nervous breakdown in front of everyone in the tavern. Bumbling her way to the ladies' room, she finally made it through the door and into one of the stalls before the tears fell. Her heart raced and, her pulse pounded so hard against her eardrums, she couldn't hear herself think. Not that her brain was piecing together any coherent thoughts.

For several long moments, Reggie stood in the bathroom stall sobbing and trying to get a grip on the tears, her breathing and her messed up life. Would she ever feel normal again?

The door to the bathroom opened and closed.

Reggie swallowed hard on the sob rising up her

throat and nearly choked. She stood still, praying whoever had entered would leave quickly, so that she could continue her panic attack in solitude.

"Reggie?" a male voice said from the other side of the stall door. "I know you're in there. Come out and talk to me."

The sob escaped her lips in a choking sound. Reggie couldn't move. Wouldn't.

In a softer tone, Sam said, "It's okay, it's just me. Unlock the door."

Reggie swiped at the tears streaming down her face and reached for the lock, pushing back the metal latch.

The door swung open.

Sam reached in and took her hand in his gentle grasp and drew her out of the stall and into his arms.

Reggie lay her cheek against his chest and let the tears flow.

He held her carefully, not applying too much pressure, but just enough to let her know he was there for her.

After a few minutes, the tears slowed, along with her pulse. "I'm sorry. I don't know what's wrong with me."

"You've been through hell. I'd think there was something wrong with you if you didn't fall apart sometimes." He tipped her chin up and stared down into her eyes. "Everything's going to be okay. We're going to find him and the ladies. No one will ever treat you like he did, ever again."

"How can you be...so sure?" she murmured between hiccups.

"Because I won't let anyone hurt you." He leaned toward her and pressed his lips to her forehead. "No man should ever treat a woman so badly. The bastard will pay." He brushed his thumb across her cheek, wiping away the traces of her tears. Then he kissed her cheek.

Reggie turned her face so that the lips kissing her cheek brushed across her mouth.

Sam captured her face in his hands and touched his lips to hers in a kiss so soft it felt like the flutter of butterfly wings.

She leaned up on her toes, wanting more, deepening the kiss on her own terms.

Still holding her cheeks between his palms, Sam let her set the pace and the extent of their kiss.

Conflicted by thoughts of what had happened at the Master's hands and what was happening now, Reggie didn't know whether she should pull away or grasp Sam's shirt and hold on. He wasn't forcing her, and he'd let go if she showed any sign of distress. Perhaps that's what made her lean closer, until her body pressed flush against his.

When she felt the hard ridge beneath the fly of his jeans, she was shocked out of the sensuous fantasy she'd fallen into and broke away. "I'm sorry. I can't. I shouldn't…" She pressed her knuckles to her mouth and fought more tears.

"No, Reggie." Sam took her hands in his and stared down into her face. "Don't be sorry. I shouldn't have kissed you. You've been through too much. Kissing you was uncalled for." He held her hands in his. "I won't do it again."

She shook her head and whispered, "What if I want you to?"

He smiled. "Then you'll have to initiate it."

She chewed on her bottom lip for a second, drew in a deep breath and let it go. "I just want to feel normal." Reggie leaned up on her toes and pressed her lips to his, closing her eyes as she did. When he didn't respond, she opened her eyes. "Only kissing you doesn't make me feel normal."

Sam chuckled and rested his hands on her waist. "I don't know whether to take that as an insult or a compliment."

She stared up at him, willing her world to quit spinning out of control. "You make me feel better than normal." Again, she stood on her toes and pressed her lips to his.

This time, his hands tightened around her waist, and his lips covered hers, giving equal pressure.

Reggie sighed, opening to him, her tongue passing between his teeth, finding and caressing his.

His arms rose up around her, pulling her close until their bodies melted together.

Reggie slipped her arms around his neck, her fingers weaving through his hair. She wanted this kiss and didn't want it to end. It was nothing like what the Master had forced on her. Kissing Sam was everything a kiss was meant to be. Soft, hard, insistent, gentle, sultry and all-consuming. When she came up for air, she didn't feel dirty, abused or like she needed to rinse her mouth with bleach.

Sam was a real man who didn't need to force a woman to make love to him. She would come willingly.

The door to the bathroom opened and a middle-aged woman wearing a waitress uniform started through, spotted them and stopped. "Oh! Sorry." She backed out of the bathroom and the door swung shut.

Sam leaned his forehead against hers. "Guess we'd better get out of here before management kicks us out."

Reggie nodded. "I'll be a minute. I want to wash my hands and face."

"I'll be right outside waiting." Sam left her standing in the bathroom.

The woman who'd walked in a moment before entered as Sam left. She laughed. "For a moment, I thought I was in the wrong place." She frowned. "Are you okay?"

"Yes," Reggie responded and gave her a weak smile.

"Are you sure?" The waitress's eyes narrowed. "You've been crying. Was that man bothering you?" She glanced over her shoulder.

Reggie laughed, the sound catching a little. "Just the opposite," She stared down at the gold band on her ring finger. "He's my…husband."

"Okay." She propped a hand on her hip. "Then why were you crying?"

With a shrug, Reggie said, "I've had a bad couple of days. He was just checking on me."

"Honey, my name is Karen. Some would say I don't know a stranger, and I take that as a compliment." The woman stared at her a moment longer. "If you're in trouble, I'll help you in any way I can. Just say the word."

With a smile, Reggie nodded. "Karen, I appreciate that. But really. I think I'm going to be okay." And she really felt like she would be. "Maybe you could answer a question for me."

"Sure," Karen said. "Shoot."

Reggie wasn't sure how to ask, so she just did. "Is there a waitress here who has seven children?"

Karen's eyes widened. "The Blue Moose has a total of eight waitresses who work full or part time. I can't say that I know any of them who have more than two kids besides me. I have three. All are grown and on their own, thank the Lord." Karen's eyes narrowed. "Why do you want to know?"

"Asking for a friend," Reggie said, her chest tightening. "I probably have the wrong tavern." She knew she didn't. More so, she knew Abe had lied about his mother working there.

Karen tilted her head to the side. "The only other restaurant in town is Al's Diner, and I don't think any of the waitresses there have that many children."

"Thanks. Sorry to bother you with my drama."

"No bother. Two of my children were girls. Drama came with the territory."

Reggie prayed their drama wasn't as destructive as what had happened to her. "You're very sweet. They must be proud to call you Mom."

Karen snorted. "They are now, but there was a time they weren't so happy with me. Curfews and groundings helped to keep them in line." The woman entered a stall, closing it between them.

Reggie turned the water on in the sink and splashed her face with cool fresh water, hoping to lessen the ravages of her tears. When she'd done all she could do to reduce the redness, she dried her face and hands with paper towels, straightened her wig and left the bathroom.

Sam leaned against the wall in the hallway, his arms crossed over his chest. When he saw her, he dropped his arms to his sides and fell in step beside her as she walked back to their table.

"Abe lied," she whispered. "His mother doesn't work here. No woman with seven children works as a waitress in town."

Sam's lips pressed into a thin line. "I figured as much."

Maggie appeared with the ordered coffee and another mug with hot water and a tea bag. "I thought you might like some hot tea," she said with a gentle smile. "It always helps me when I'm feeling low."

"Thank you." Reggie dipped the tea bag into the mug of hot water. When the water was dark enough, she removed the bag and stirred in a teaspoon of sugar.

Sam drank his coffee black. No sugar.

The waitress returned to take their orders of the night's special: chicken fried steak, mashed potatoes and green beans. She was back several minutes later with their food and a smile. "*Bon Appétit.*"

"I can't eat all of this," Reggie said, guilt knotting her gut. "I find it hard to sit here like nothing is wrong in the world when I know there's so much that needs to be fixed."

"Eat what you can. We'll take the rest home."

Reggie knew he'd said home as part of their cover story, but the word from his lips gave her a warm safe feeling she wrapped around herself like a blanket. For the next half hour, they ate, making comments about the weather, comparing it to what it was like in San Diego. As if they'd just moved to Eagle Rock from there. Again, all part of their cover.

Occasionally, Sam reached across the table and caressed the hand with the wedding ring on it. A blast of electricity would zing through her system every time he touched her.

Reggie wondered, if they weren't putting on a show would Sam find her attractive. Or would he think, like she did... that she was too damaged and dirty to want to be with her?

She tensed, a terrible thought occurring to her. What if she was pregnant? What if that bastard had gotten her with child? And what man would want to take on the responsibility of being a father to a rapist's spawn?

Though she'd hate the thought of having a lifetime's reminder of her captivity, Reggie wouldn't terminate the pregnancy. It wouldn't be the child's fault the father was a criminal.

Sam's big hand covered hers. "Stop it."

She looked up, startled. "Stop what?"

"You're getting all worked up again. You can't change the past, but you're in full control of your future." He leaned closer and whispered. "Don't let him take one more minute of your life from you."

She nodded, realizing her pulse had picked up and her breathing had become ragged. "You're right." Willing her body to calm, she closed her eyes, drew in deep, steadying breaths and let them out slowly. Finally, she opened her eyes and gave Sam a tight smile. "I'm okay."

By then, several of the tavern's customers had risen from their tables and headed toward the exit.

Maggie came by with their check and laid it on the table. "Do you need anything else?"

"No, thank you." Sam handed her his credit card.

When Maggie turned toward the cash register, she bumped into one of the men on his way out, knocking into his arm.

The man dropped the jacket he'd been carrying and let out a stream of curse words.

His voice struck a chord in Reggie's memory. Her heartbeat went from zero to one hundred and twenty in a second. She fought between spinning to see who the man was and ducking beneath the table. She turned slowly, but all she could see was the man's back as he bent to retrieve his coat.

"Oh, I'm sorry," Maggie was saying as she bent to help.

"Damned clumsy woman," the man said loud enough everyone in the tavern heard and turned toward him. He straightened and stormed out, muttering more curse words

Maggie shot a glance around at the people staring at her and the door where the man had stormed out. "Sorry, folks."

A hand closed over Reggie's. "What's wrong?" Sam asked.

Reggie turned back to him, his voice one she would always associate with warmth and safety. She shook her head. "I had a déjà vu moment."

"Whatever it was, you're as white as a ghost," he curled his fingers around hers. "What brought it on?"

"That man's voice. The one Maggie bumped into." Her gaze captured his as the full import of what she'd just heard hit her. "He sounded just like the Master."

CHAPTER 11

Sam was out of his seat in the next second. "Stay here," he commanded and wove his way through customers to get out of the building. Once he was outside, he searched the darkness for the man who'd bumped into Maggie.

Unfortunately, that man had been one of about ten people who'd left the tavern at the same time. Several vehicles were pulling out of the parking lot at the same time. A sedan, two trucks and two SUVs. Sam couldn't tell into which vehicle the man who'd bumped into the waitress had gone. He tried but failed miserably at memorizing six different license plates. He gave up and hurried back into the tavern, afraid to leave Reggie alone any longer than he had to. What if the Master had doubled back to grab her and take her out the back?

Reggie met him in the front entryway, standing

145

back in the shadows, out of sight of the street beyond the door. "Did you see where he went?" she asked, her voice shaking, her body trembling.

Sam shook his head. "No. There were too many people, and they were already driving away by the time I got outside."

Maggie found them by the door. "Oh, good, you're still here. I thought you'd left without your credit card." She held out Sam's card and a receipt. "I need your signature."

He scribbled his name at the bottom and added a sizeable tip. "Maggie, that man who bumped into you..."

"I feel so bad. I'm not usually so clumsy." She grimaced. "He did have a potty mouth though. I'm so sorry you had to hear that."

Sam shook his head. "I'm not worried about that. Do you know who he is?"

Maggie shook her head. "I've only seen him in here one other time. He sat by himself and didn't talk to anyone except to order his food."

"Did he pay with a credit card?" Reggie asked.

Maggie's brow creased. "I don't know. One of the other waitresses had his table tonight. I can ask. Why?"

"I'd like to know his name," Sam said. "He looked familiar, like someone I know."

Maggie stood on her toes, looking back into the tavern. "Wait here. I'll ask Janice if she knows him, or if he used a card to make his purchase. I'll be right back." She took off, weaving her way through the tables and people coming and going.

From where Sam stood, he could see her talking to the other waitress. They walked to the register by the bar and opened the bottom drawer. After a moment or two they both looked up, shaking their heads.

Maggie returned a moment later, her lips pressed into a line. "I'm sorry, but Janice thinks he paid with cash. She checked the register, but most of the receipts were people she knew. If you see the man, please let him know I'm super sorry for knocking into him." Maggie went back to work, waiting tables.

"God, I hope he wasn't here to target any of the women in Eagle Rock," Reggie said. She slipped her arm through the crook of Sam's elbow and leaned into him. "Let's get out of here."

Sam led her out the door and settled her into the passenger seat of his truck. He untied Grunt from the light post and held the back door open for him to jump inside, closing it behind him. When Sam climbed into the driver's seat, he cast a glance her way. Though her face was still pale, she'd stopped trembling. "Do you really think it was him?"

She shrugged and grimaced. "It could have been him. Or I could have been too sensitive to a similar voice." Reggie wrapped her arms around herself and looked at him, her brow twisted. "Is this how it's going to be? Me jumping at every voice or worrying that he's in the same room as me, and I can't recognize him?"

"No. We're going to find him and put him away for good." Sam shifted the truck into reverse, backed out of the parking space and headed toward the White Oak Ranch. "We're getting closer. I just know it's only a matter of time before we catch up to him."

Reggie didn't say it, and she didn't have to. It was only a matter of time before the Master hurt those women. Maybe even killed them. They had to hurry before it was too late.

"I feel like he's close," Reggie said, twisting the ring on her finger. "Like we could have been the ones to bump into him instead of Maggie, if we'd left a couple minutes earlier."

"We'll find out what Hank's guys came up with and put it together with what we learned today. Maybe it will lead us straight to him."

"God, I hope so." Reggie sat quietly for the rest of the drive to Hank's ranch.

No sooner had Sam hit the intercom button at the gate, then Swede's voice came over. "Sam, glad you made it here. See you in the war room."

The gate slid open, and Sam drove along the winding drive to the ranch house. He helped Reggie out of the cab and up the steps to the front door where Sadie and Hank met them.

"Come on in," Hank said.

"Have you had supper?" Sadie asked.

"We have."

"Good. Then we can get right down to business." Hank led the way down the stairs into the war room.

Sam squeezed Reggie's hand reassuringly as they descended into the basement and came to a halt behind Swede.

Three other people were in the room with him. A big man with a barrel chest, broad shoulders and a thatch of thick brown hair. A man with black hair and piercing blue eyes stood beside him, the same height, also broad-shouldered, but nearly as thick as the bigger guy. Beside him stood a woman whose head came up to his shoulders and had dark red hair.

As Sam and Reggie entered the war room, the redhead flashed her bright green eyes at them. "You must be Sam and Reggie." She held out her hand. "Molly Greenbriar. FBI."

Reggie shook her hand, a frown forming on her brow. "I'd forgotten you were with the FBI. I was just thinking that you were Kujo's woman, accompanying him on the river."

The black-haired man beside Molly stuck out his hand. "I'm Joseph Kuntz, affectionately known as Kujo." He rested a hand at the small of Molly's back. "Actually, I'm with Molly, aka Special Agent Green-briar. She's the one with all the training."

Molly elbowed him in the gut. "Don't listen to

him. He's prior Delta Force. And yes, we were on the river all day with a drone."

Sam held out his hand and shook Kujo's and Molly's. "I'm Sam Franklin, the new guy with the Brotherhood."

"Good to know you," Kujo said. He motioned toward the dog at his feet. "This is Six, retired military war dog extraordinaire.

The Belgian Malinois lifted his head briefly and laid it back down on his paws.

"I hear you adopted one as well," Kujo said.

"I did," Sam reached down and let Six sniff his hand. "Grunt's out on the porch keeping an eye on the squirrels."

Kujo turned to the big guy beside him. "Oh, and this is Bear."

"Nice to know I rank after the dog. Tate Parker," The big man engulfed Sam's hand in his larger one. "Glad to have you aboard. You can call me Bear."

Sam turned to Molly and Kujo. "Which way did you go at the fork? North or South?"

"We took the south fork. Why?" Kujo asked.

"We ran into a local who knows the area fairly well. He said the north fork has the high cliffs. Reggie jumped from the cliffs into the river. Did you see any cliffs beside the river on the south fork?"

Molly exchanged a glance with Kujo. "Not anything over a couple meters."

Sam turned to the man at the computer keyboard. "Swede—"

"Pulling up the contour map now." His fingers danced across the keyboard, and the monitor flashed an image of a contour map with squiggly lines depicting the elevation of the terrain. He scrolled across the map, following the blue line of the river to the point where it split into two around a long, broad island that stretched for several inches across the map. Based on the legend, the island was approximately a mile long and a quarter of a mile wide.

Swede zoomed in on a grouping of contour lines that converged into one with tick marks pointing toward the river.

Sam pointed. "There. Abe said it was on the north branch of the river. It has to be the one Reggie jumped off. Bring up the satellite map of that area."

"On it," Swede said. A moment later he had the satellite map displayed beside the topographical contour map. Matching the sizes, he zoomed in on the cliff then backed out slowly. "The problem is that there are so many tall trees, unless the houses have been cleared around them, you might not see them."

Sam studied the satellite image, his brow furrowing. Finally, he pointed to the image. "Isn't that the place where you said one of the registered sex offenders lives?"

Swede nodded. "Thomas. But his cabin was too

small to have a basement big enough to hide five women in individual cells."

"I checked with the parole officer today, asking about Ogletree, Thomas and Knowles."

Reggie cringed. "What reason did you give them?"

Bear said, "I told him I was concerned about them being in this area as my fiancé was a rape victim. I wanted to know if they were reporting regularly to their parole office and if he'd had any issues with any of them."

"And?" Sam prompted.

"They are all playing by the books," Bear said. "So, I drove out to Knowles and Ogletree's houses while they were away at work in Eagle Rock and had a little snoop around." He shook his head. "Nothing. Like you said, the cabin at Ogletree's place was small with an even smaller basement beneath it. No women in there."

"You broke in?"

"Not really," Bear shrugged. "The place was unlocked. And Knowles's place was a mobile home. No basement and no outbuildings with basements. Just a veritable junk yard filled with discarded truck chassis."

"What about Thomas?"

Bear nodded. "I drove out near to his place and went in on foot to keep from being seen or heard. The man lives like a hermit. Just him. He lives in what I'd call a cottage. It has a cellar, but it's not on the side of a hill, and the cellar was really small from what I could see through a dirty window. Again. It wasn't on the side of a hill.

"Maybe we're focusing on the obvious people and not on the real culprit," Hank said. "Who owns the land directly north of the cliff?"

Swede brought up the county plat map of the area from the state website and scrolled over the areas slowly. "This is going to take some digging. I'll look into these owners and run some background checks. Likely, it will take into the night."

Sam shot a glance toward Reggie. "We could use showers and sleep."

"I'm okay," Reggie said, though her face was pale, and the shadows beneath her eyes had darkened.

"You might be, but I could use a few hours of sleep after tromping around in the woods." Sam held out his hand. "We should head back to the cabin."

"Nonsense," Sadie said. "It's late. You two can stay here. We can loan you some clothes to wear for the night and Swede will have information for you first thing in the morning." She looked to Hank.

"Sadie's right," Hank said. "There's plenty of room for all of you to stay."

"If you really don't mind, I'd like to do that," Reggie said. "The cabin's comfortable but a little distant from the computer and the information it can generate."

"Agreed," Sam said. "But I was serious, you need some rest."

"I know my limits." Reggie squared her shoulders as if ready to fight. Then she gave him a twisted grin. "And you're right. I'm on the edge of them." She turned to Sadie. "I feel bad accepting anymore clothing from you when you sent over so much to the cabin."

"Oh, don't worry. I've got more clothes than I'll wear in my lifetime. Clothing designers send me stuff all the time, hoping I'll represent their lines. Come on. I'll find something suitable for sleeping." She turned to Hank. "Make sure your guys have what they need, will you?" Her gaze went to Molly. "Come on, us ladies have to stick together, or these men will run all over us."

Kujo laughed. "You obviously don't know Molly very well. She can hold her own."

"I'm sure she can," Sadie said.

Molly followed Reggie and Sadie up the staircase out of the basement.

Sam remained behind, not sure why he felt as if he was missing something important. Like the woman he'd been with fulltime for more than twenty-four hours. She was growing on him. So much so, that he didn't like it when she wasn't within sight.

"Hank, Reggie and I ate at the Blue Moose Tavern this evening. When we were finished and waiting to pay our bill, Reggie thought she heard the voice of the man who'd held her captive. He was on his way out the door when she heard him. By the time I got outside to check it out, he was gone. I'm not sure that information buys us anything since we didn't see him, but it might prove that he's from around here, if that was in fact the man who'd kidnapped all those women."

Hank's face set in grim lines. "All the more reason to catch this guy. None of the women of Eagle Rock or the surrounding areas are safe as long as he's running free. I'd like to issue a warning to the area."

"But we can't," Sam said. "Not until we find him and the women he's currently holding captive."

Hank nodded. "In the meantime, we can only hope and pray he doesn't kidnap anymore women."

CHAPTER 12

SADIE, carrying Emma in her arms, led Reggie and Molly up the stairs to the second level of the ranch house and into the massive bedroom she shared with her husband, Hank. She kept walking to the other side of the room where a door led into a walk-in closet larger than Reggie's apartment in Bozeman.

Molly whistled. "Holy hell, I could live in here."

Sadie blushed. "Hank went a little overboard designing the closet. He seems to think a movie star needs a closet big enough to house a small nation." She grinned. "I have to admit, I love it. And Emma likes playing in here while I'm getting ready in the morning.

Emma flapped her arms and leaned over.

Sadie set her on the floor and closed the door to keep her from wandering out. "Let's see. You both need something to sleep in." She shot a glance from

Molly to Reggie with raised eyebrows. "Unless you sleep in the buff."

Molly shook her head. "I rarely sleep in the nude. My mother told me I should never go to sleep in anything I don't want to stand outside in, in case of a fire."

Reggie chuckled. "Same." Though she'd slept in the nude for over two weeks while being held in the basement of the Master's house, wrapped only in a threadbare blanket he'd sparingly provided. The memory brought her back to that bad place she never wanted to return to.

Sadie broke into her morose thoughts by handing her a soft pink, baby doll nightgown. "This should fit you. It's short, but it covers the bases." She gave Reggie's arm a squeeze. "And pink is cheerful and will compliment your strawberry-blond hair. You look like you could use a little cheering up. I can't imagine what you went through, and I won't pretend I do. But you're safe here, and Sam will make sure you stay safe."

Sadie handed Molly a mint green nightgown, also short and sassy. "Sorry, ladies, Hank likes me in baby doll nighties or nothing at all." She winked.

"Suits me," Molly said. "I don't like things that tangle up around my legs at night. I used to sleep in gym shorts and a T-shirt while at the academy at Quantico."

Sadie sifted through a drawer and pulled out

silky bikini panties. "You'll need some of these." She added them to the top of the nightgowns the two women held. Moving to another drawer, she pulled out two loose cashmere sweaters, one in a deep forest green, another in powder blue, handing the green one to Reggie and the blue one to Molly. "I take it you're okay with the jeans you're wearing?"

Reggie nodded, grateful for anything. Until she returned from the dead and could visit her apartment in Bozeman, she was at the mercy and kindness of Sadie. "Thank you for putting me up in your home."

Sadie waved her hand. "Oh, please. I love having company out here. You're doing me a favor by staying." She wrapped her arms around Reggie. "I'm just so sorry we've met under such dire circumstances. But I'm not sorry we met."

Tears welled in Reggie's eyes. "Thank you." She stepped back and turned to admire the racks of dresses hanging behind her.

Emma had found her way in among the long dresses and tugged at their hems, playing hide-n-seek among the folds.

"Come here, you rascal." Sadie swooped in and gathered the happy child in her arms.

"Mama, play," she said in her little baby voice.

Reggie's heart squeezed hard at the love she saw in Sadie's eyes for the little girl.

One day…she hoped and prayed she would have a little girl like Emma to hold in her arms.

"Let's show these ladies to their rooms. I'm sure they're tired and could use a good night's rest, like you." She kissed her daughter's chubby cheek and led the way out of her closet and down the hallway to a door on the left. "Molly, you can have the blue room. It has its own en-suite bath. The bed is already made. If you need anything, just let me know."

"Lord knows, I need a shower after being on the river all day. I'm sure I smell like fish and sweat." Molly thanked Sadie and entered the room, closing the door behind her.

"Reggie, I'm putting you in the room near the end of the hall. Sam will have the room beside you, since he's in charge of keeping you safe. Not that you have anything to worry about here. Hank had the entire ranch wired with security cameras and alarms. No one can get in without triggering some really loud and annoying sirens. Seriously, I thought I'd lose my mind when they were testing them." She flung open a door. "You have the yellow room. It's one of my favorites. Yellow reminds me of sunshine and makes me happy. I hope it does the same for you."

"I'm sure it will. Thank you."

"Again, if you need anything, let me know." Sadie glanced down at Emma. "Say night-night, Emma."

The little girl waved her hand and gurgled, "Night-night."

Reggie waved at Emma as Sadie closed the door between them.

Left alone in the yellow bedroom, Reggie's body sagged with weariness. She'd held it together all day, because she refused to give up on finding the women. Now, alone in a stranger's house, the weight of the world seemed to settle on her shoulders.

Before she collapsed from exhaustion, she carried the clothing Sadie had equipped her with into the bathroom, started the water in the shower and stripped off the clothes she'd worn on their hike through the woods that day.

Naked again, she shivered and faced the mirror. She didn't look much different from the woman who'd had a life in Bozeman, working at the office she'd set up to manage the various businesses and investments her father had left to her and her mother in a trust. Maybe she was a little thinner, with darker shadows beneath her eyes, but not much had changed on the exterior.

Inside, she would never be the same again.

Reggie stepped beneath the shower's spray and let the water run down over her skin. She didn't try to scrub the filth of the Master from her body. No amount of scrubbing would ever get what he'd done to her out of her memory. Only time would heal that broken place inside. As Sam had said, she couldn't let him rob one more minute of her life from her. The best revenge would be to live a happy life, in spite of what he'd done—after she made sure he didn't hurt any other woman, ever again.

Reggie squeezed shampoo into her palm and worked it through her hair. It smelled like spring and wildflowers. She rinsed the suds from her hair and body, applied conditioner and rinsed again. By the time she left the shower, she was more relaxed and smelled like a completely new person.

After quickly drying with a large, fluffy white towel, she dressed in the soft pink nightgown and panties. Finding a new brush in one of the drawers, she ran it through her hair, smoothing the tangles. Feeling so much better, but tired, she walked into the bedroom and switched on the lamp on the nightstand.

That's when she noticed a door at the side of the room. She walked to it and pressed her ear to the panel.

Sounds of movement on the other side made her pulse quicken.

Sadie had said Sam would sleep in the room beside hers to keep her safe.

Warmth spread throughout her body at the thought of Sam on the other side of the paneled door. After spending the past twenty-four or more hours with him, Reggie found she missed him. He'd made her feel safe, even while they'd been tromping through the woods.

Perhaps he'd showered and was climbing into bed

right now. Did he sleep in shorts and T-shirt? Or was he one of those men who didn't wear anything to sleep in?

Her core heated, desire pooling low in her belly. How could she be aroused when she didn't know the extent of the damage that monster had done to her? She could be infected with a sexually transmitted disease. She could be pregnant. If she hadn't had to play dead, she'd have had a rape kit run on her and reported directly to the police. They'd need every bit of evidence possible to convict the man and send him to jail for the rest of his life.

Reggie leaned her cheek against the cool panel. She wanted to be with Sam, to have him hold her in his arms.

A sharp rap startled her and made her cry out. Reggie jumped back from the door and pressed a hand to her chest.

The doorknob turned and opened. "Reggie?" Sam poked his head through the door. His chest was bare, and his hair was damp. Random droplets of water stood out on his shoulders.

Reggie swallowed hard but couldn't get words past the knot in throat.

Sam frowned and stepped through the door. "Are you okay?"

He wore black boxer briefs that did little to hide the ridge of his cock beneath the fabric.

She shook her head.

He entered the room, gripped her arms and stared down into her eyes. "Sweetheart, what's wrong?"

"I can't…" She shook her head again. She wanted to say she couldn't be with him until she had all the answers, but that would assume he wanted to be with her. Instead, she finished with, "I can't sleep."

"Do you want me to stay with you until you go to sleep?"

Her brow furrowed. "I'm not usually so wimpy."

"You're not wimpy at all." He drew her into his arms. "You escaped a madman. I'd say that took a huge amount of courage."

She lay her cheek against his bare chest, inhaling the clean, fresh scent of him. "Courage didn't get me out of there. I'm not that brave."

"Yes, you are." Sam tipped her chin up and stared down at her. "You knew what he'd do if he caught you digging, but you dug anyway."

"Because I was afraid of what he would continue to do to me, if I didn't get out of there."

"And yet, you're trying like hell to go back."

"I have to. I can't abandon the others." She rested her hand on his chest, her fingers curling ever so slightly into his skin. He felt so good, so right, she couldn't stop touching him.

"Come on. I'll tuck you in."

God, she didn't want to move. She wanted his arms to remain around her for as long as she drew air into her lungs. He was her lifeline in a sea of uncertainty.

When she made no move toward the bed, he bent, scooped her up in his arms, carried her across the room and laid her on the mattress.

She clung to him, her arms wrapped around his neck. "I can't let go. Please, don't make me."

He chuckled. "Okay, then. But let me lie down beside you."

She scooted over, making room for his big body on the bed.

He laid down and gathered her again in his arms. "You know you're safe here in Hank's house."

She nodded. "My brain tells me I'm safe, but my heart…not so much."

"I'll stay as long as you need me," he reassured her.

"And if that's all night?" she whispered.

He sighed. "If it's all night, I'll be here." Sam brushed a strand of her damp hair behind her ear. "Just know, it'll be a struggle."

She frowned. "I'm sorry. If you don't want to, you don't have to stay."

He snorted. "That's just the problem. I want to… too much." He kissed the tip of her nose and frowned. "Sorry. I said I wouldn't initiate a kiss again, and yet, I did."

"Don't," she said, touching a finger to his lips.

"Don't what?"

"Don't be sorry." She cupped his cheek in her

palm and pressed her mouth to his. "I want you to kiss me," she said against his lips. "I want you to hold me. But not because I want you to." She brushed her thumb across his lip. "Because you want to."

"Oh, baby, I want to hold you. I want to do more than hold you. But after what you've been through, I won't go beyond holding you. Not until we see this through and get you the medical attention you need."

She nodded, her heart swelling in her chest. "One good thing about all this is that I got to meet you." Reggie snuggled into his side and laid a hand across his chest. "I'll sleep for now, but tomorrow...we're ending this chase."

Sam laid a hand over hers. "Damn right, we are."

Though her pulse raced, and she wasn't in the least bit sleepy, she lay still next to him, knowing she could get up and leave whenever she wanted. Because she could leave, and Sam wouldn't stop her, Reggie had no desire to move. Her desire grew for this man, giving her hope that the abuse she'd suffered wouldn't affect her attitude toward her future sexuality.

Unfortunately, the women she'd wanted to help were being forced to spend another night with an insane man. She'd hoped that by escaping, she could get back to them with the help they needed to be free of the Master.

Hang in there, she prayed. *Help is coming.*

Eventually, her heartbeat slowed, and exhaustion

claimed her. With Sam's arms wrapped around her, her ear pressed to his chest and the steady beat of his heart marking time, Reggie drifted into a troubled sleep.

She woke in a dark cell, the scent of damp earth and urine filling her senses. She felt her way around the walls until she came to the door. It had no handle on the inside. Only someone on the outside could open it. Reggie tried digging her fingers into the gap between the door and the doorframe, but the fit was too tight. Back around the room she moved, feeling for something, anything she could use to pry the door open. All she found was a thin blanket and a tin cup.

Sounds of someone sobbing drifted in beneath the door. Heart wrenching wails echoed down the hallway beyond the door, adding pressure to the weight of hopelessness on her chest.

"We'll never get out," a voice called. "We'll die here."

"No," Reggie said. "Help is on the way. Someone will come."

"It'll be too late," another female voice cried. "Too late."

No. It couldn't be. Sam and Hank would send help. They would get them out.

"They won't find us in time."

"Yes, they will." Reggie argued. "They're coming."

Footsteps sounded on the stairs leading down into the dark, dank cellar. The crackle of the cattle prod sent a flash of fear through Reggie's body.

"He's coming for you," a voice called out. "He's angry that you got away."

Reggie backed away from the door until she felt the cool damp wall of her cell against her naked back.

The footsteps stopped.

Her breath lodged in her lungs.

The door swung open, and a large man in a ski mask stood silhouetted against the dull yellow lantern hung on the wall behind him.

Reggie screamed.

CHAPTER 13

"HEY, REGGIE." Sam sat up and smoothed a lock of strawberry-blond hair away from her forehead. "Sweetheart, wake up. You're having a bad dream."

She tossed her head back and forth on the pillow. "No...please...no," she cried, tears slipping down her cheeks.

Sam's heart constricted. He didn't like seeing her in pain. If he could, he'd take it all away from her. "Reggie," Sam said, more insistently. "Wake up. It's just a dream."

Her eyes popped open, and a whoosh of air left her lungs. "Sam? Dear Jesus. Sam!" She flung her arms around his neck and pressed her face against his bare chest. "I didn't think you'd get to us in time. He was there." Her words drowned in sobs. "He'd come to get me."

"Sweetheart, it was only a dream." He leaned

against the headboard, holding her in his arms, his hand sliding up and down her back. "Just a dream."

"It was so real. The voices. The smell… Him." Her body shook.

Sam knew exactly what she was talking about. He still had dreams of battles where he'd lost friends. In his dreams, he could still smell the dust, hear the cries of his teammates and taste the blood. "I know, baby. I know just how real it feels. But you're not in that cellar. You're here in Hank's house, with me."

Her hand on his chest clenched and unclenched, finally smoothing over his skin. Reggie drew in a ragged breath and tilted her head up to look into his face. "Thank you," she said.

"For what?" He chuckled and pressed his lips to her forehead for a brief kiss. "I didn't do anything."

"You found me on the river. And you came in time to save me from my dream."

"Agreed, I was on the river at the exact right moment to find you. But I've been here all night. You just had to come back from your dream. I didn't save you then."

She snuggled closer, still staring up at him. "I'm afraid to close my eyes again. He's waiting for me. I can feel it."

"Then stay awake with me. We can talk or play cards."

She shook her head. "You shouldn't have to give

up your sleep for me. I'll be okay. Please, go back to sleep." She started to pull away.

Sam tightened his hold, ever so gently. "I'm awake. I wasn't sleeping very well anyway."

She seemed reluctant to move any further away.

Sam was glad. He liked holding her. But that short pink nightgown was doing crazy things to him. The longer she pressed her scantily-clad body up against his, the tighter his groin grew. He'd be in physical pain before long.

"Why were you awake?" she asked, her head resting on his shoulder.

"I couldn't sleep. There was a beautiful woman in my arms, keeping me awake and aware." He smiled down at her. "I told you it would be a difficult night for me, but I'm here for you."

"I'm sorry," she said.

"Don't be. You didn't ask to have a man kidnap you. It's not your fault you're having nightmares because of what he did to you." He brushed his lips across her forehead. "I'm glad I could be here to help."

Her eyes narrowed, and her lips twisted. "Were you this kind as a Navy SEAL?"

Sam stiffened. "Only to my teammates, women, children and dogs."

"Do you have nightmares about the battles you fought?"

"All the time," he answered, his words barely a whisper.

She snorted. "Aren't we a pair. I'm a wreck, and you're kind of broken, too."

This time, he gave her a lopsided smile. "That's why we work well together." Settling back against the padded headboard, he sighed. "What do you want to do until daylight? Talk, sing, play cards? Although, I have to warn you, I can't carry a tune. My friends liken my singing voice to the braying of a donkey."

Reggie chuckled. "We can sleep," she suggested. "I think I can close my eyes now without seeing him."

"Are you sure?" Sam asked.

She nodded.

"Give it a try. I'll stay awake in case you slip back into that dream."

She nodded, took a deep breath and closed her eyes. For a moment, there was silence. "See?" she said. "No bad guys. No bad dreams." She slipped lower into the sheets, her nightgown riding up her thigh to expose a shapely hip covered in lacy pink panties.

Sam swallowed a groan and pulled the sheet and quilt up over her and him to hide the evidence of his growing desire. He slid lower in the bed and held her close until her breathing deepened, and she slept.

Sleep for Sam didn't come. He wanted to hold Reggie so much closer but knew he couldn't. Only time and patience would see her through the damage that bastard had done to her. To get his mind off the beautiful woman in his arms, his thoughts turned to what they had to do when the sun rose, and they could get out to the river and backtrack to the house Reggie had escaped. He hoped they weren't too late to help the women trapped beneath it. He figured freeing the others would go a long way toward helping Reggie recover from her own memories and lingering demons. They had to find them soon.

Sam curled his hands into fists.

They would.

HE MUST HAVE FALLEN ASLEEP, because the next thing he knew, sunlight was pushing through the slits of his eyelids, urging him to rise.

Reggie lay with her head tucked into the crook between his shoulder and chest, sleeping soundly. The color had returned to her face, and the dark shadows had faded significantly.

Her eyelashes fluttered. She opened her eyes and stretched, her hand encountering his body.

"Hey," he said. "You seem to have slept pretty good."

She nodded and smiled up at him. "I did. No dreams that I can remember."

"That's a step in the right direction."

"Yes, it is. I'm ready to start this day and make it count." She sat up, remembered she was wearing a tiny pink nightgown and blushed. Her hands went to the sheet, and then paused. "I guess it's a little late to cover up, considering I slept with you all night."

"You do what makes you comfortable." He laced his hands behind his neck and winked. "You can think of me as furniture."

"You're anything but furniture, Sam Franklin." She settled back down beside him and slipped her hand over his chest. "Why didn't I meet you before...?"

"You didn't need me then," he answered. "And it's likely you won't need me after we wrap up this case." He lifted her hand and kissed the tips of her fingers. "Did you ever consider that? I mean, we barely know each other."

"I know enough about you to know I like you." Reggie frowned, her gaze on the hand he held in his. "Is it that I'm just a case to you? An assignment?" Her frown deepened as she gazed up into his eyes.

"No. Actually, how I feel is far from thinking of you as an assignment. I'm afraid I'm failing at my first job as a Brotherhood Protector."

"How so?"

His jaw hardened, and he looked at the window in front of him. "First, we haven't found the bastard who hurt you." When he glanced back down at her, his face and voice softened. "Second, I'm pretty sure that I'm not supposed to fall for my client."

Her cheeks reddened, and she swept her tongue across her lips. "And are you?"

"Going to find the bastard?" He nodded, purposely answering the wrong question. "You're damn right we are."

He liked it when the color in her cheeks deepened. "No," she said. "I meant are you falling for your client?"

He tilted his head as if considering her question. "Hmm. I'm lying in bed with her. She's beautiful. And I haven't tried to make love to her when my entire body and soul is begging me to." He nodded. "Yeah. I'd say I'm in grave danger of falling for her." He sat up and brought her to a sitting position with him. "You, or at least the idea of what we could be together, is the primary reason I left the military. I want a life. A wife. A passel of children and a place to call home." He gathered her hands in his. "I know it's too soon to hit you with all that, but that's what went through my head all night long while I held my client in my arms, watching her battle nightmares and PTSD."

She stared at their hands. "What if I'm not ready for all that?"

"I wouldn't expect you to be ready. Like a physical wound, the emotional wounds take time to heal. Sometimes, those take more time than the physical ones." He lifted her hands to his lips. "When I know what I want, I'm a very patient man. And I'm persistent. But don't let me scare you. You might not want what I want. It's my job to show you what a great guy I am. And if that doesn't work, no worries. I'll come up with another plan." He winked. "Now, let's get this day started. We have some women to free and a lunatic to catch and put away for the rest of his life."

Reggie snorted. "You make it sound like it's all by the numbers," she said swinging her legs over the side of the bed, a smile pulling at her lips. "Find the bad guy. Rescue the women. Put the bad guy away." She stood and clapped her hands together. "And done." Her smile faded. "God, I hope you're right. I hope we find him and bring him in without anyone else being hurt."

Sam stared at her standing in the soft morning light, the shape of her body silhouetted beneath the frothy pink nightgown.

His groin tightened. "The sooner we get started, the better," he said and got out the other side of the bed. He headed for the other room, his back to her so that he didn't embarrass or scare her with the jutting evidence of desire. "I'll be ready in less than ten minutes," he called out over his shoulder.

"I'll be ready in five," she responded.

Sam closed the door between them and groaned. Ten minutes might not be enough time in a cool shower to bring his desire under control. He hurried to the bathroom, stripped and turned the water on cold. The shock of water that originated as snow on the mountaintops hitting his engorged cock brought him back to reality.

He couldn't think straight if he was always thinking about making love to Reggie's beautiful body. He had to focus on the other women whose dire situation was desperate and sobering.

Stepping out of the shower, Sam had renewed his determination to bring this manhunt to a close. Today was the day. It would be done.

Then perhaps he could get on with his life, and Reggie could start healing. Sam wanted to be there to help her through the process, but she had to be in a place to heal herself. With the Master still on the loose, she wouldn't have the closure she needed.

REGGIE DRESSED in her borrowed jeans and sweater. She slipped the shoulder holster on and buckled it in place, then slid the .40 caliber into it. The weight felt unnerving at the same time as it comforted her. As soon as they found the Master and freed the women, she would return to her apartment and her own wardrobe. She'd buy her own pistol and get her concealed carry license.

Her life in Bozeman seemed so far away. Had it really only been a little over two weeks since she'd been kidnapped?

For the first time since that fateful night, she felt better. More like the old Reggie, though she knew the old Reggie would be no more. She couldn't go back to being the carefree young woman who couldn't conceive of being kidnapped and raped multiple times. For the rest of her life, she'd be wary of dark alleys, strangers and men she didn't know.

As soon as she could, she'd enroll in self-defense classes. If she ever had children, she'd have them trained in self-defense from the moment they could walk.

She shivered at the thought of having a child kidnapped and tortured as she'd been tortured. Knowing the kinds of monsters that existed, could she bring another child into this messed up world? She thought of Hank and Sadie's daughter Emma. That precious baby.

Reggie had always wanted children, but now...? She wasn't sure she could.

After she'd dressed, combed her hair and brushed her teeth, she pressed her ear to the door between her room and Sam's. She could hear the water in the shower still running. Rather than wait for him, she decided to go downstairs and help out in the kitchen. With extra guests in the house, there would be added work to prepare breakfast for them all.

When she arrived in the kitchen, she found Hank and Kujo in control of cooking breakfast. "There's coffee in the pot, milk and juice in the refrigerator," Hank said. "Help yourself. Sadie's changing Emma's diaper. She should be back in a second."

"What can I do to help?" she asked.

"How about setting the table with utensils and glasses?" Hank suggested. "Kujo and I have the cooking under control."

Kujo pulled piping hot biscuits from the oven and set the pan on a trivet.

Hank returned his attention to a pan of fluffy yellow scrambled eggs and a griddle lined with pancakes.

Sadie sailed into the kitchen with Emma in her arms. "Good morning, Reggie. I hope you slept well last night."

Heat climbed up Reggie's neck and suffused her cheeks. "I did. Thank you."

"After breakfast, we'll meet with Swede in the war room and bring you and Sam up to speed on what we've discovered during the night."

"Did you find the house?" Sam asked from the doorway to the kitchen.

Reggie's insides quivered at the sound of his voice, and warmth spread throughout her body. She'd never had that kind of reaction to any man in her life. Why was Sam so different? Was she experiencing some kind of hero worship because he'd saved her life? Would it fade after the Master was captured and rotting in prison? She turned to see Sam wearing his jeans like they were a natural part of his body. And the black T-shirt he'd put on to cover his gorgeous chest stretched over the muscles, leaving little of his impressive physique to the imagination.

Her body on fire with desire, Reggie turned to the refrigerator, opened the door and stood in the cool air, praying the heat would abate before she had to face the man again.

"What did Swede find?" Sam asked.

"Not a whole lot, but maybe something," Hank said. "Upon close inspection of the satellite images, he thinks he found the hard lines of a roof through the trees in a couple places near the cliffs and dirt roads leading in from the highway. They bear checking into."

"Is there an address from the road, leading into the property?" Sam asked.

"Not that we could find. We suspect it's an old abandoned house." Hank met Reggie's gaze. "Do you remember if there were electric lights in the house?"

Reggie closed her eyes and pictured the cellar, the stairs and the house above. It had the musty smell of an older home with dry rotted joists and moldy walls and furniture. "I remember there not being many lights and lots of shadows. It was really creepy. And there was a steady hum of an engine when the Master was there."

"Maybe a generator?" Sam asked.

Reggie nodded, opening her eyes. "He always hooked a battery-powered lantern on the wall outside our cells before he opened the door and took one of us up to the big house. And he left it there until he brought us back." A cold chill rippled down her spine as she shut the door to the other memories of being inside that house.

Sam took her hand. "Thanks."

"Does that help?" she asked.

Hank nodded. "It could mean he's off the grid. Which means, no registered address with the power company or the tax office. It also makes the house harder to find. Especially, if the trees and vegetation have grown up around it."

"But you said Swede found evidence of buildings out there," Reggie said.

"He did," Hank said. "Let's hope one of the buildings is the house we're looking for." He glanced at Sam. "The other alternative is that the rooflines are old deer camps or covered deer stands hunters placed in the trees."

Swede joined them for breakfast and discussed the potential of hidden buildings in the forest.

"There's another thought we might need to be prepared for. Montana has several active groups of survivalists. They live off the grid in remote locations."

Hank's face was grim. "And they don't like folks walking into their camps uninvited."

"That's right," Swede said. "They might shoot first and ask questions later. And they have plenty of places to hide the bodies."

When the conversation turned morbid, Sadie shooed them out of the kitchen and down to the war room, claiming she'd heard enough negativity for a lifetime.

In the Brotherhood Protectors' basement war room, the men continued the conversation. Two more men arrived, introducing themselves as Taz and Chuck. They joined in on the planning and potential outcomes.

The more theories they came up with, the worse Reggie felt. "If there's a chance those women are out there, I'm willing to risk running into a survivalist's camp to find them. As far as I could tell, there was only one man at the house where I was held. But he had two Rottweilers who'd just as soon rip you apart as look at you. So, whoever goes in with me needs to be prepared for them."

Sam was shaking his head before she finished speaking. "You're not going in."

Reggie lifted her chin and met his gaze. "I have to. I promised to get them out of there. I know the layout of the house enough to get to the cellar."

Sam frowned. "He could be armed. I can't put you at risk of being shot."

"You're not putting me at risk," she said. "I'd be putting myself at risk. And it's a risk I'm willing to take. Besides," Reggie lifted her chin higher, "if you don't take me, I'll go by myself. I have to see this through."

Sam started to say something, but Hank stepped into the conversation with, "We'll cross that bridge when we come to it. For now, we need to recon the areas Swede has identified. If we find a house on a hill, we report back. No one goes in until we have a team assembled. Understood?"

Sam, Kujo and Swede all nodded, used to taking orders.

Reggie slowly nodded. They were right. She couldn't go in alone. She needed Sam, Hank and his team to get those women out alive. And they needed the element of surprise on their side.

"I'm sending Bear, Taz, Kujo and Chuck out to scout the area. Molly, you're welcome to join them. But I wouldn't alert your counterparts in the FBI, just yet. We don't know if the kidnapper has connections. The rest of us will wait until we hear back from them. However, they'll remain in place until we have the team assembled and ready to make the move. Sam, you and Reggie can stay here, or head to town. I don't suggest you drive on the highway out to the locations. The fewer people out that way, the better. He might be watching the roads. They aren't major highways.

Hank had his team gear up with satellite phones, two-way radios, headsets and bulletproof vests. Each man selected his choice of weapon and ammunition.

"Reggie, I know we fit you with a .40 caliber

pistol. Did you have a chance to test-drive it?" Hank asked.

She shook her head. "No, we didn't. Do you happen to have a taser or a stun gun?" she asked. "I might feel better about using something that won't kill me if I mishandle it."

"I do have a taser, and you might also like this." He held up a small canister that would fit easily in the palm of Reggie's hand.

"What is it?" she asked.

"Mace." He held it up. "All you have to do is point it in his face and press the top. It'll blind him long enough for you to get away."

Reggie shoved the canister into the pocket of her hooded jacket and placed the taser in the other pocket. She patted the .40 caliber pistol in the holster beneath the jacket and felt a little ridiculous at being armed to the teeth. Then again, she was going after the man who hadn't hesitated to deploy a taser on them, shocked them with cattle prods and kept them drugged so much that they couldn't fight back.

If she had to, Reggie would use the full force of every weapon she had to stop him from ever doing that to anyone ever again.

Everyone headed out of the ranch house. Hank walked with them. "I want you to take a trailer with you and several four-wheelers. Park the trailer a couple miles away from the locations identified by

Swede. Split up and go in on the ATVs until you're within a mile of each."

"Got it," Kujo said. "And we'll move in on foot from there."

Bear drove the truck around to the barn where they hitched a trailer to the back of it. One by one, they loaded the four-wheelers onto the trailer. It was decided that Molly would ride double with Kujo. His dog, Six, would be able to run alongside them through the woods until they reached the point at which they'd ditch the ATV and continue on foot.

Reggie's pulse quickened as they finished loading the ATVs. Kujo, Molly, Bear, Taz and Chuck loaded up into the four-door cab of the pickup, and they left the barnyard with the coordinates Swede had given them of the places he'd identified from the satellite images.

"I have business in town," Hank said. "I'll be at the sheriff's office to talk to him about another case one of my guys is involved in. I'll keep my ears open for anything out of there and my satellite phone clipped to my belt. Where will you two be?" he asked of Sam and Reggie.

Sam turned to Reggie. "We'll be in town as well. Since the highway is on the other end of town from this ranch, we might as well be as close as we can get without actually driving out there."

Reggie gave a tight smile, glad Sam hadn't decided to leave her behind with Sadie.

"I'll get Reggie geared up with some of your communications equipment before we head into town," Sam said. "Should have done it when we got the others wired."

Hank nodded. "Good. I'll see you later." He kissed Sadie and Emma, and then climbed into his four-wheel-drive pickup and headed for town.

Swede and Sadie walked with Reggie and Sam back into the house, down the stairs to the war room and into the arsenal.

Sam gave Reggie a two-way radio headset and showed her how to use it. After she'd successfully communicated with him from the other room, he helped her fold it up and stuff it in the pocket with the mace. Then he filled a bag with two bulletproof vests, a couple of flashlights and night vision goggles.

Swede approached Reggie, carrying what appeared to be a necklace with a pendant hanging from the chain. "Wear this at all times. If for some reason you're separated from Sam, we can find you with this. It has a built-in tracking device we can follow using this." He handed a GPS tracking monitor to Sam.

"What if I want to keep track of Sam?" Reggie asked, arching an eyebrow.

"Trust me," Swede said. "He'll find you. And you're the potential target. Not him."

Swede made a good point, but Reggie would have liked to be able to track Sam if she should lose sight of him. The mere thought of being out of Sam's sight made her knees weak and her body tremble.

Reggie squared her shoulder and fought the fear threatening to overwhelm her. She'd clawed her way out of that hell without any help. She would do whatever it took to get the others out alive. If it meant going in alone, she would. Her hand rested on the .40 caliber tucked beneath her jacket. This time, she wouldn't let him hurt her. And she'd kill him before she let him hurt anyone else. God, she wished she'd had time for Sam to show her the basics of how to use the gun. Somehow, she'd make it work.

CHAPTER 14

REGGIE FOLLOWED Sam out to his truck.

He held the door for Reggie, and then Grunt, and placed the equipment bag on the back floorboard. Once they were settled, he climbed in and drove to Eagle Rock.

As they passed the sheriff's station, Reggie noted Hank's truck parked there. If they ended up needing help, Hank was in the right place to get it. That was reassuring on a day when anything could happen. Or not.

Reggie sat silently in the seat beside Sam, her fingers twisting in her lap.

Near the opposite end of town from where they'd entered, a woman driving a minivan was parked at an odd angle in front of an antique store, the hatch on the back of her van open and several bags of groceries scattered across the ground.

Reggie could see immediately that the minivan's left rear tire was flat, and the woman was struggling to lift a tire out of the back.

"We have time," Reggie said. "We should stop and help."

Sam had already put on his blinker and was pulling over.

"My father made sure I knew how to change a flat tire as soon as I was old enough to drive on my own. He said no woman should ever be stranded on the side of these Montana highways because she didn't know how to change a flat." Reggie glanced across at Sam. "Want me to do it?"

Sam smiled. "I'm sure you're amazing at it, but I'd feel better if you stayed in the truck with Grunt."

Reggie didn't argue. Sam had agreed to take her on the mission to find the Master. If he wanted her to stay with Grunt, she'd stay with Grunt while he changed the tire.

The lug nuts on the woman's flat tire proved to be a challenge. From what Reggie could hear through her open window, they'd been put on with a torque wrench, making it nearly impossible to dislodge. Fifteen minutes into changing the woman's tire, Sam only had half of the lug nuts off, and he'd worked up a sweat.

Grunt paced across the back seat of the pickup.

Reggie was getting anxious, thinking the guys might have reached the drop-off point by now and would be mounting the ATVs for the next leg of their reconnaissance mission. She glanced at the satellite phone, praying for it to ring. She crossed her fingers, hoping they found the house and reported in soon. Then they'd be on their way to finally free the other women.

She stared out the window at the minivan, willing the lug nuts to loosen already.

Grunt whined behind her and paced faster, back and forth across the truck seat.

"I know. They're taking too long." Then she had another thought. "Do you need to go outside?"

The dog stopped moving and stared at her. Then he barked and went to stand at the door, waiting for her to let him out.

"I guess when you gotta go, you gotta go." Reggie glanced at Sam bouncing on the tire iron, working hard at loosening the lug nuts and making slow, painful progress. She didn't want to bother him. He needed to get done with the tire changing as soon as possible.

Which meant she'd have to take Grunt for a walk to relieve himself.

She grabbed the lead, straightened her wig and slipped out of the passenger seat. As soon as she opened the back door, she realized her mistake.

Grunt leaped to the ground and took off before Reggie could snap the lead on his collar.

Sam had just dropped the tire iron, the clatter

covering the sound of Reggie's curse. She closed the truck door gently and ran after Grunt. The animal turned down an alley between the antique store and an insurance agency. He'd probably seen a cat and was hot on its trail.

"Grunt!" she called out. What was the word Sam used to make the dog stay? "Grunt, *bleib!*"

Too late, the dog had rounded the back corner of the building and disappeared out of eyesight and hearing.

A sharp yelp sounded from the back of the building.

Reggie ran after Grunt, afraid he'd tangled with the wrong cat and had gotten himself hurt. Running as fast as she could, she barely slowed to take the corner.

As she came around to the back of the building, she saw Grunt lying on the ground, motionless. "Grunt?" she called out and rushed toward him, her wig slipping off the back of her head.

A figure detached from the shadows, leaped out and flung a bag over her head.

Darkness blocked the daylight. Reggie couldn't see anything, and her arms were trapped by the coarse fabric of the bag and the strong arms wrapped around her. Hands reached beneath her jacket and relieved her of the .40 caliber pistol. They patted her sides and removed the taser as well. Then she was lifted off her feet, carried several yards, and then dumped into what could only be a trunk.

As soon as the arms around her let go, she shot up and tried to roll out of the back of the trunk, screaming as loud as she could. The sound was muffled by the sack over her head as she fought to push herself free from the back of the vehicle.

No. No No. This was not happening again.

"You shouldn't have run away," a voice said. The sound filtered through the sack but was no less familiar. He shoved her back into the trunk and tried to shut it on her.

Reggie fought even harder, bracing her feet on the trunk lid, pushing up to keep him from lowering the heavy metal and locking her in.

She couldn't let him take her. She'd made a promise to herself that she would return to free the others, not to return to become a prisoner once again.

"Hey, leave her alone," a young voice called out.

Hope spurred Reggie on. She kicked at the trunk lid and aimed blindly at the hands attempting to close it.

The Master lurched as if he'd been hit broadside. He slammed the trunk closed before Reggie could get free.

Complete darkness surrounded her. She finally worked the fabric sack from her head and shoved it aside.

"Let her go!" the youth's voice sounded again.

Something hit the trunk hard, and then the sound of heavy footsteps pounded around the vehicle. A door opened and closed with a sharp slam. The engine revved, and the car jerked forward.

Reggie screamed as loud as she could and kicked the trunk lid, hoping to get the attention of anyone the car passed. At first moving slowly, the car picked up speed. Reggie assumed it had reached the edge of town and now sped along the highway, back to the big house, the dark, dank cellar and the end of her freedom—and probably her life. For surely, he wouldn't let her leave again. Not alive.

She didn't feel as sorry for herself as she did for the women she'd failed to free of this sociopath. When he stopped and got her out of the trunk, she had to make it count. He'd taken her taser and pistol, but he'd missed the little canister of mace. Reggie had one shot at escape. She needed to be accurate and deliberate. Most of all, she'd better make it count. If the Brotherhood Protectors were out there, she prayed they'd found the Master's house. She might be able to buy some time, but between the Master and his two Rottweilers, it wouldn't be much. Reggie doubted she'd make it to the river a second time.

She clutched the small canister of mace in one hand and the necklace with the GPS pendant in the other.

Come on, Sam. I've never needed you more.

Though she'd been raped and tortured, and it could happen again, Reggie wasn't ready to give up on life.

Sam had shown her that she wasn't just damaged goods. He found her attractive, even though another man had left his mark on her mentally and physically. He'd shown her that not all men were monsters like the Master.

Though she'd only known him for a short time, Reggie knew Sam was special. A man of honor and integrity. He would never hurt a woman or take advantage of her when she was broken. She wanted the chance to get to know him better, to learn to trust men again, because of him.

She wanted to have a man make love to her... when she was ready. And she wanted that man to be Sam.

A sob rose up her throat.

Reggie swallowed hard, forcing it back down. For now, she was on her own. She couldn't fall apart and wallow in the stench of fear. She had to keep her cool and fight back the only way she knew how. With every fiber of her being.

SAM HAD SWITCHED the tire and was tightening the lug nuts on the spare when a familiar voice called out behind him. "Sam!"

"Abe?" Sam turned to find Abe, the teenager, staggering toward him, his cheek bruised and blood running down his face from a cut over his eye.

"You gotta come quick." He staggered and fell into Sam's arms. "Your lady… He took her."

Sam's gaze shot to the truck where he'd left Reggie to wait for him with Grunt. The back door was open, and neither Reggie nor Grunt were in the truck.

Abe grabbed his arm and tugged him toward an alley. "Your lady, he took her. And your dog…" He shook his head. "I think he's dead." Tears blended with the blood on the boy's face. "I tried to stop him, but he was bigger. I couldn't…" He shook his head as he limped down the alley, hurrying to the other end.

Sam left him and ran ahead. When he reached the back of the buildings, the only sight that greeted him was that of the German Shepherd lying on his side as still as death and a brown wig.

"He was here. The man in the ski mask. His car was here." Abe stood near Grunt, turning in a three hundred and sixty degree circle, clasping his hands to his head. "He threw her in the trunk…and he got away."

Sam's heart slammed against his ribs. "What did the car look like?"

"It was dark. Black, I think. Four doors. But he put her in the trunk." Abe dropped to his knees next to the dog. "He's dead, isn't he?" He looked up at Sam. "I couldn't help either of them."

As Sam approached the dog, he pulled out his cellphone and contacted Hank. "The Master got Reggie. Call in the big guns. We have to find her before he kills her."

"I just heard from Kujo," Hank said. "He and Molly saw a dark sedan pass them on the highway, heading in the direction of their designated location to investigate. They were on foot with more than a mile to go, I'll let them know."

Sam ended the call, leaned over Grunt and watched his chest for any sign of life. After a few moments, he noticed Grunt's chest expand. Then it did it again. He was breathing.

Relief filled Sam. He scooped the dog into his arms. "Is there a vet nearby?"

Abe pointed. "A block that way. I used to hang out and walk the dogs there before Mom got sick." He led the way to the vet's office less than a block away. The vet was in and took Grunt into surgery immediately.

Sam said he'd be back, but he had to leave.

Abe followed him out. "Are you going to save Ginnie?" he asked running alongside Sam as he raced back to his truck and the satellite phone he'd left in the console.

"I'm going to do the best I can."

"I'm going with you," Abe said.

Sam shook his head. "Where I'm going could be dangerous. I need you to go home and take care of your siblings until I can get back to you."

"My sister, Lacey, has them. She can watch over them until I get back."

"No, you don't understand. If you come with me, you might get hurt. You might not get back to your family. And I know for a fact that they depend on you. You can't afford to have something bad happen to you." Sam put a hand on the young man's shoulder. "Your duty is to them. I'll take care of my lady. You've already been a big help. Please."

Abe nodded. "Okay. But I feel responsible for Ginnie, too. I should have stopped him."

"You couldn't, but you did your best. Now, I have to go."

Abe took a step back, squaring his shoulders. "You know where to find me if you need help."

"I do. And I'll be back. That's a promise." Sam climbed into the truck, shifted into drive and pulled onto Main Street, heading west into the Crazy Mountains and following the road that paralleled the north branch of the river. He pressed the accelerator to the floor, hoping to catch up to the sedan that was taking Reggie away from him. What if the Master didn't take her to the house where he'd been holding the other women? What if he killed Reggie and dumped her in a ditch along the side of the road? Sam might never find her.

Then he remembered the GPS tracker. Still blasting along the highway at an insane speed, he fumbled in the bag he'd packed to find the tracking device.

For a moment, he took his foot off the accelerator, allowing the truck to slow to a more manageable pace. Switching it on, he waited for it to warm up and find Reggie in the vastness of the Montana landscape.

For what felt like forever, the screen remained dark. Then it blinked to life and displayed a bright green dot. It was moving. It had to be Reggie. She had to be alive.

Sam pressed his foot down hard on the accelerator. She wasn't more than five minutes in front of him.

He held the steering wheel in a white-knuckled grip as he maneuvered the curves, increasing his speed as he came out of them. If the master had shoved Reggie into his sedan alive, he hadn't had time to stop and kill her. As long as they were still moving, Reggie had a chance. Once they stopped, all bets were off.

All the more reason for Sam to catch them before that happened. He pushed harder on the accelerator, screaming around the curves, the bed of his pickup swinging wider, almost pushing him into a spin. He righted the truck, slowed slightly on the next turn and raced on.

The satellite phone rang in his lap. He fumbled

with it to answer, keeping one hand on the steering wheel.

"You just passed Kujo and Molly," Hank said. "They're at their site. It's an old barn. They're high-tailing it back to the ATV and will continue on the road to catch up with you."

"I've got Reggie on the GPS tracker. They're still moving. I'm maybe four minutes behind them."

"Stay on them," Hank said. "Bear, Taz and Chuck haven't checked in yet. Wait. That's them now. I'll call right back."

A quick glance at the tracker assured him Reggie was still on the move, but they were slowing.

His pulse raced, and his heart squeezed hard in his chest. Reggie's life hung in the balance of a few short minutes.

If the Master stopped, he could kill her in less than a second. Sam could be too late.

He leaned into the steering wheel, urging the truck to go faster, the curves to be straighter and Reggie to live long enough for him to save her.

The satellite phone rang.

Sam grabbed it and held it to his ear. "Talk to me, Hank."

"Bear and Taz are on foot, closing in on a dilapi-dated two-story house that appears to have been abandoned."

"And?" Sam prompted, impatiently.

"They just saw a car drive into a lean-to on the other side of the structure. A dark, four-door sedan."

"Tell them to shoot the bastard," Sam entreated.

"They can't see him from their vantage point. They're moving around the perimeter now."

"They can't wait. He might kill her."

"They don't have a clear line of fire. Got your radio headset?" Hank asked.

"Yeah."

"Wear it. You don't want to shoot each other."

He reached for the earbud, fumbled to slip it into his ear and switch it on. "Got it on," he reported.

"Good," Hank said. "I'm not far behind you. Don't do anything crazy. Remember, we're better as a team. We can't let this guy get away because we were too hasty in our decisions."

Sam gritted his teeth. "I'm three minutes out, closing in. If they don't get to him first…I will. He will *not* get away."

CHAPTER 15

"GET OUT!" the Master said, his voice a menacing growl.

Reggie blinked at the flashlight beam shining down into the trunk and her eyes. Gripping the canister of mace in her palm, she waited, not wanting to blow her only chance because she couldn't see his face. The mace had to hit him square in the eyes to blind him long enough for her to make her escape.

She sat up and braced her free hand on the edge of the trunk

"Get out!" He reached a cattle prod into the trunk and hit her with the charged end.

A surge of 50,000 volts blasted through her, sending her falling back, her body jerking. The hand with the canister automatically opened, and the mace can rolled out.

"Hurry up, bitch, or you get it again."

"I can't move when you zap me with that," she said through clenched teeth, her hand patting the floor, searching for the little canister. Just when she thought she'd lost it, her fingers touched the smooth metal. Curling her fingers around it, she gripped the side of the trunk and pulled herself up.

Before she could get her balance, the Master grabbed her hair and yanked her out onto the ground.

She landed on her hands and knees, her knuckles slamming against the gravel. But she didn't let go of the little canister. And now that she was out of the trunk and her eyes had adjusted to the dim light of the lean-to he'd pulled the car under, she could aim and put her plan into action.

"Get up!" he yelled. He raised the cattle prod, swinging it toward her.

Reggie lurched to her feet, spun and faced the bastard. "Don't hit me again," she said, through clenched teeth.

"I'll do whatever the hell I want. You've caused me more than enough trouble. Now, I'll have to get rid of you and the others."

Before he could hit her again with the business end of the cattle prod, Reggie raised her hand and sprayed mace straight into eyeholes of his ski mask.

The man screamed and clutched at his eyes with his empty hand, while swinging the cattle prod in the air in a wild attempt to zap her.

Unfortunately, to make her escape, she had to either go through him to get out into the open or go into the house through the door behind her. Armed with the cattle prod, even if he couldn't see clearly, the Master could hit her in one of his wildly swinging moves.

Taking her chances on the house, she lunged for the door and yanked it open. Reggie dove into the kitchen, turned, closed the door and twisted the lock. Since the top of the door was a window, it wouldn't hold him long. Reggie ran out of the kitchen and through to the old sitting room.

The muffled sound of dogs barking came from somewhere else in the house. Reggie prayed they were locked in another room and wouldn't be able to come out at tear her apart.

What little light that filtered through the filthy windows cast shadows on the ragged furniture, making it difficult for her to weave her way through what once had been a happy home, but was now a house of horrors. She remembered the sagging, dusty sofa, the faded wingback chair and the fireplace that smoked whenever he chose to light a fire in the grate. She remembered the path he'd taken her from the stairs in the hallway, through the sitting room and into the bedroom where he'd raped her and the other women.

Her anger fought against fear. She wasn't drugged

now. Her head was clear, and she'd be damned if he'd get away with hurting her ever again.

Glass shattered, and the door slammed open in the kitchen.

Her heart in her throat, Reggie searched the room for a weapon. She'd used as much of the mace as possible the first time around. It was only meant to be used once to allow her time to get away. The sitting room had no doors to the outside. Reggie passed through to a hallway that had once been a front entryway with a large wooden door. She ran to the door, gripped the handle and pulled hard. It didn't budge. Not even a little. She twisted the deadbolt and pulled again. Nothing.

The sound of boots hitting the wooden floor sent her across the hall into another room devoid of furniture, with moth-eaten curtains hanging on the long windows too thick with dust and dirt to see through. A broken wooden chair lay on its side in a corner, covered with cobwebs.

Reggie ran for the chair, grabbed it and swung it at the closest window.

The glass shattered, leaving razor-sharp shards jutting up from the window frame. Using the chair, she wiped at the shards, knocking them loose.

The footsteps sounded in the entryway, crossing the hall. From all the noise she was making, he'd know which room he'd find her in. Reggie threw down the chair, swung her leg over the windowsill and screamed.

Sharp pinpricks pierced her back and electrical shocks burned through her nerves.

She fell back on the floor, completely incapable of moving to defend herself.

No. No. No.

The Master entered the room, pulled zip-ties from his back pocket, rolled her over and secured her wrists together behind her back.

Reggie knew from having experienced being tased before that that the effects lasted between five and thirty seconds. If he didn't secure her legs, she still had a chance of getting away. Any chance was better than none. As long as he didn't carry her down the basement before the paralysis wore off…

One thousand and one. One thousand and two.

The Master, lifted her, flung her over his shoulder and took her to the hallway where he unlocked the door that led into the cellar below.

One thousand and three. One thousand and four.

Reggie could feel some of the feeling returning to her fingertips and toes, but she still couldn't move her arms or legs.

He descended the steps one at a time, slowed by the effort of carrying the deadweight of her body.

One thousand and five. One thousand and six.

Come on muscles. Work!

One thousand and seven. One thousand and eight.

At the bottom of the steps, he paused in front of a wooden door, fumbling with a key on a keychain clipped to his belt loop. A battery-powered lantern hung on a hook on the wall. Sobs sounded behind other doors along the narrow passageway.

They were still alive. Relief flooded through Reggie, and determination swelled in her chest. She had to get them out.

One thousand and nine.

Reggie could wiggle a toe, and then another. Her fingers tingled and moved.

One thousand and ten. One thousand and eleven.

The Master shoved the key into the lock and flung open the door to a dark, dank, earthen cell.

As if a veil lifted on her muscles, Reggie could feel when the paralysis lifted, and her legs would answer her brain's command to move. She kicked out, slamming her feet against the doorframe. She pushed so hard it took the Master off balance. The arm he'd had clamped around her legs loosened enough she twisted and fell out of his grip, crashing to the floor.

The Master reached for the door and tried to swing it closed.

Reggie rolled to her knees, bunched her legs beneath her and rushed him like a linebacker going for the quarterback. Her shoulder hit him in the gut, sending him flying backward. He landed hard on the floor. Without the use of her arms and hands, Reggie couldn't slow her momentum and crashed to the floor on top of him.

He lay for a moment, the wind knocked out of him, unmoving.

Reggie rolled off him, pushed to her feet and raced up the stairs.

"Bitch!" he yelled and came after her, clomping up the stairs in his boots.

Thankfully, the door was still open.

Reggie ran through and straight for the window she'd broken out. It was her only hope. He wouldn't have time to reload the taser. If she could get to the window first, she'd make it.

Down the hallway, into the empty room and across rotting wooden floor she flew. She didn't care that she would be going through the window head-first or that she had no way of breaking her fall. All she knew was that she had to get away from him, or she'd die. She didn't slow but kept moving, using all her momentum to throw herself through the opening. Her body sailed through. And as if in slow motion she saw the windowsill pass by. Her head ploughed through an overgrown bush, and her legs had almost cleared the room. She was almost free when a hand reached out and snagged her ankle.

Her flight came to an abrupt halt, and she crashed down into the bush, the hand on her ankle feeling like an iron shackle.

Reggie kicked at it, but another hand captured her other foot, making it impossible for her to fight his hold. She was slowly dragged over the branches and the windowsill, back toward the house and into the room. Her only hope left was that Sam and the Brotherhood Protectors would find her. She drew in a deep breath and screamed as long and loud as she could.

Sam had the windows down in his pickup as he turned down the rutted path leading to the location where the green light designated on the GPS tracking device. When the ramshackle house came into view, he heard a piercing scream.

Rather than slow his truck, he raced toward the house and skidded to a stop at the foot of the rotted steps leading up to a front door. He drew his weapon from his shoulder holster, threw open the truck's door, leaped out and ran up to the front door of the dilapidated house. Boards had been nailed across the entrance. It would take him too long to pull them free. By then, Reggie would be dead. He ran around the corner to where a covered shed had been built, butting up against the side of the house. A dark sedan had been parked beneath the rickety shed.

Another scream sounded from inside the house.

"Sam, you copy?" Bear's voice sounded in his headset.

"Roger." He slipped between the car and the house. A door stood open, the window busted out of it.

"Taz is on the other side of the house. Our bogey just pulled Reggie in through a window. He's coming in from that direction. I just made it around the perimeter to the side with the shed. I'm coming in behind you. Don't shoot me."

"Roger. Going in."

"I'd say wait for backup," Bear said, "but it sounds like she's in trouble. Go!"

Sam stepped through the door. Glass crunched beneath his boots, but he didn't slow. Sounds of a struggle came from a room deeper inside the house. He hurried forward, his pistol in front of him.

He found his way through a kitchen and a sitting room, what little light left in the sky barely making it through the grimy windows. When he emerged into a hallway, he found Reggie, her arms trapped behind her, her back pressed up against a man wearing a ski mask who held a pistol pointed at her head.

"Come one step closer, and I'll shoot the bitch," the man warned.

Reggie's gaze was wild and piercing. "Sam. Don't listen. Shoot him. He's going to kill me anyway."

"You don't want me to kill her," the Master said, his mouth drawing up on one side beneath his mask in a sneer. "I saw you two together in the tavern.

You're sweet on her. You don't want her pretty face splattered all over your hands."

"Sam," Reggie said, her tone calm, insistent, resigned. "Shoot him. If you don't, he'll kill the others."

Sam's heart pinched in his chest. "I can't. I risk hitting you."

She sighed and gave him a weak smile. "Please, Sam. You have to do it for the others. For me. I promised I'd get them out. And you can't let him get away."

"Shut the hell up," the man said and poked her temple hard with the tip of his pistol. "You've been nothin' but trouble. You weren't even that good to screw. Why, I should..."

"Shoot her?" Sam said, leveling his gun at the man's chest. He couldn't pull the trigger yet. If he did, the bullet would pass through Reggie before it hit the man in the heart. But he could be ready. If anything changed...if Reggie were to get away from him...he'd take that shot. The man had to die. He was pure evil. He didn't deserve to live, much less to breathe the same air as Reggie. "You know if you shoot her, you're a dead man. I'll take great pleasure in filling you with holes. But I'd hit you where it hurt a lot before you died. I'd make you feel every bit as much pain as you've inflicted on the women you've abused."

Sam's anger took him a step closer. "Men who

prey on women aren't men. They're cowards who can't find a woman to love them because they're too weak and pathetic."

"Shut the fuck up," the man bit out. "Do you think I care if she dies? I don't. She means nothing to me. Go ahead, like she said and shoot me. You're not going to let me live anyway. Think I care if I die?" He snorted. "I'm tired of hiding. Tired of living where people treat me like shit. Go ahead and shoot me. Go ahead." He tightened his hold on Reggie, his finger shaking on the trigger. "But I'm taking her with me."

Reggie shook her head. "You bastard. You don't deserve to get off that easy."

Just then, he saw Reggie shift. Sam wasn't sure what she was doing, but she dipped slightly, her arm flexing behind her.

The man behind her squealed and hunched over, the barrel of his weapon moving from the side of her head.

At the same time, Reggie bent in half, giving Sam the opening he needed to take the shot.

He did, hitting the man in the shoulder of the arm holding the gun. His arm jerked back, the weapon flying from his fingers to skitter across the floor.

Reggie let go of her captor's balls that she'd been squeezing and staggered forward into Sam's chest. He circled his free arm around her, his gun held steady on the man in the ski mask.

The Master grabbed his arm and dropped to his knees. "Go ahead. Kill me. You know you want to."

Sam felt his frame tremble. The urge to do just that was strong. "Oh, man, I do. But I want to see you suffer more. What's the going sentence for someone who has held a woman captive and raped her on multiple occasions? Multiply that by the number of women you've done that to." Sam snorted. "You'll be in prison until you die. And maybe someone there will use you as his bitch and rape you, too."

Bear entered the room, his gun drawn. "I see you got everything under control. Want me to take over?"

"Please," Sam said. "Reggie and I have more to do." He nodded toward the man in the mask. "Let's see who the bastard is who had to hide behind a mask to feel like a man."

Bear reached over and plucked the ski mask from the man's head.

The guy beneath had salt and pepper hair and appeared to be in his mid-forties.

Hank entered the room from the hallway, his gun drawn, followed by Taz, Molly, Kujo and Six. "I see you've found Timothy Thomas. I believe you've not only committed multiple violent crimes, but you've also violated the hell out of your parole." Hank holstered his weapon. "The sheriff is on his way out to collect his prisoner. Have you found the women? Are they alive?"

Reggie turned. "If you'll get me out of this, I'll lead the way."

Sam pulled his pocket knife out of his jeans and sliced through the plastic.

"First, give me your jackets," Reggie said.

The men stripped out of their jackets and handed them to Reggie. She motioned for Molly. "They'll be more comfortable seeing women first."

Molly nodded.

Reggie bent and ripped the keychain off Thomas then led the way down the stairs into the cellar, opening the doors one at a time.

The women inside fell into her arms, crying. Their naked bodies were bruised and dirty, but they were alive.

Sam watched as Reggie and Molly wrapped each one in a jacket and passed them over to the Brotherhood Protectors to carry out of the basement and the house, up into the fresh air.

Ambulances arrived along with several sheriffs' vehicles.

The ladies were loaded into the ambulances first and carried off to Bozeman, where they'd be evaluated, have rape kits run on them and be treated. Their families would be notified, and they'd start the long road to recovering from the horror they'd endured at the hands of their captor.

"You, too," Sam said, nodding toward the ambulance. "You need to be checked over by a doctor and have a rape kit done on you as well. Every voice needs to be heard. All the evidence needs to be collected. That man needs to stay in prison for the rest of his life."

"I'll go, but I'd rather you took me," she said. "That's if you don't mind."

"Sweetheart, if you wanted to ride in the ambulance, I'd ride with you." He pulled her into his arms and held her close. "I don't want to let you out of my sight ever again."

She laughed, feeling better by the minute. Then a thought occurred to her. "Grunt. What happened to Grunt?"

The sheriff chose that moment to walk up to Sam and Reggie. "You must be Sam Franklin, Hank's new agent. I'm Sheriff Barron."

Sam shook the man's hand.

The sheriff turned to Reggie, his smile as gentle as the hand he held out to her. "And you must be Reggie McDonald. From what Hank tells me, you're quite the hero." He held her hand in his and patted it softly. "I'm sorry you had to go through what you did. But I'm glad you had the chutzpah to get yourself out of it and bring us to the others. It's an honor to meet you."

"Thank you," Reggie said, her eyes suspiciously bright. A single tear slid down her cheek. "I don't see myself as a hero, though. I only did what I had to."

"Well, you did a hell of a job." He let go of her

hand and turned back to Sam. "I just got word from one of my deputies who knows the veterinarian. Your German Shepherd was stunned by a blow to the head, but he'll live. He's got him resting at his office until you can collect him. No hurry, if you want to see this amazing woman to Bozeman for a checkup."

Sam let go of the breath he'd been holding, a rush of emotion filling his chest. "Thanks for letting me know."

Reggie slipped an around his waist and leaned her cheek against his chest. "We should go. I want to be back in Eagle Rock before it gets too late. Grunt needs you."

Sam chuckled and held her close. "I came to Montana to start living my life and maybe find someone I cared enough about to share it with me, someone who might care enough about me to consider being a part of my life." He gave her gentle smile. "Here it's been less than a week, hell less than a few days, and I think I've found the woman of my dreams." He tipped her head up and stared down into her eyes. "Don't let me scare you off. I'm willing to wait until you're healed and ready to think about dating. But I hope I can be first in line when you decide you're up for it."

She laughed. "I'll pencil you in on my calendar." Reggie leaned up on her toes. "I wouldn't want to miss out on my very own hero."

"Oh, baby, you've got that all wrong." Sam shook

his head. "The sheriff nailed it. Sweetheart, *you're* the hero. I was just along for the ride."

"Well, take me to the doctor. I want to know I'm okay physically." She cupped his cheeks in her palms and brushed her lips across his. "I'm thinking I might be recovering sooner rather than later."

"Darlin', no rush. I'll be ready whenever you are." He slipped her into the crook of his arm and escorted her to his pickup.

As they drove away from the house, Reggie looked back at the structure and shivered. "To think, someone used to call that home a long time ago."

"It's a shame that Thomas used it like he did. The best thing that could happen would be for someone to bulldoze it and plant a tree in its place."

Reggie turned to face the front. "That's how I will think of it. As if someone planted a tree there. No more looking back. The future is in front of me. I'm not giving another minute of my thoughts and memories to the past."

Sam reached across the console for her hand and held it on the hour-long drive to Bozeman.

He knew it would take more than a promise to let go of the past. Reggie would be plagued by flashbacks and bad dreams until they faded. But knowing her tormentor was locked away for good would bring a measure of closure to that chapter of her life and allow her to build a future.

Sam realized it was the same for him. He'd come

to Montana weighed down with grief and regret over his last mission that had gone so badly.

Reggie was right. The future was in front of him. He couldn't change the past, and he wouldn't wallow in it. And if he had to wait a month or a year or two for Reggie to recover enough from what she'd gone through, he would. She was worth it. The woman would risk her life to help others, including him. The least he could do would be to help her find a new normal. Hopefully, with him.

CHAPTER 16

"Sam? Are you ready? Everyone is waiting in the van." Reggie stood inside the front door of the big old, drafty house they'd bought for a song three years ago and yelled up the stairs to her husband. She shifted her six-month-old baby girl to her other hip.

"I'm coming. I can't believe you wanted me to wear this old thing." He came down the steps dressed in his formal dress blues with colorful ribbons covering his left chest and a shiny gold trident flying above them.

Reggie's heart fluttered as it always did when she saw her husband coming toward her. He was as handsome now as the day he'd pulled her out of the river. And he was such a good father to their eight children.

He stopped in front of her and let her tug at his necktie.

"You know you wanted to wear it," she teased. "Abe's never seen you in your dress blues. He'll be so proud to have you there when he swears into the Navy."

"He should have gone into the Air Force," Sam muttered.

Reggie snorted. "As if you'd let him."

"It's not as hard."

"Abe's up for it." Reggie smiled. "He's going to be amazing at whatever he does. He's had you as a role model."

"That boy had it in him before he met me. We just gave him the opportunities he needed." Sam kissed the top of her head. "Did you hear from Hank?"

"Sadie called. They left fifteen minutes ago. They'll be in Butte before us, if we don't get a move on."

"Anyone else coming?" he asked.

"Swede, Bear, Boomer, Chuck, Trevor, Gavin. Hell, it would be easier to ask who's not coming." Reggie smiled up at him. "They're all so proud of Abe and want to give him a good sendoff."

"Well, let's get going. We wouldn't want Abe to be late for his swearing in." He reached for his daughter.

Reggie backed away with her. "No way. She'll burp up milk all over your jacket."

"I'll take my chances."

"No, you'll drive," she said.

"You know, you're a lot easier to get along with

when you're naked." He swept her into his arms and planted a long, satisfying kiss on her lips.

"Sam! You're impossible." She laughed and swatted at his arm.

Samantha hooked her daddy's arm and made the transition to him like a little monkey.

Reggie shook her head, giving up. She could never be mad at Sam. He was everything she'd ever wanted in a friend, lover and husband. They'd been in perfect agreement over adopting Abe and his six siblings when they'd finally found out that their mother had died of an overdose, leaving them orphaned. The state had had one condition—Sam and Reggie had to be married in order to adopt all seven of the children.

That hadn't been a problem at all. The Brotherhood Protectors had experience putting on weddings and were quick to pull it together. The wedding had been perfect with the children participating in the ceremony and agreeing to love honor and cherish each other for life.

With Timothy Thomas safely ensconced in jail for the rest of his life, and the women he'd terrorized free and recovering, life had only gotten better.

Abe had graduated from high school at the top of his class. He'd preferred to defer college in lieu of following his adopted father's footsteps into the Navy. He'd even been training seven days a week to Navy standards, borrowing the pool at Hank's to build his swimming skills and strength.

Sam was so proud. The rest of the Brotherhood Protectors had taken a personal interest in Abe's training, all volunteering to run, swim or weightlift with him.

Lacey was in her last year of high school and already had a full ride scholarship to Montana State University.

The other children had taken to Sam and Reggie as if they'd been starved for love and attention. And they'd all been ecstatic when baby Samantha had come along.

Reggie still had an occasional nightmare, but those were few and far between. She was happier now than she'd ever been in her life and wouldn't change a thing.

Sam tucked Samantha into her car seat and tightened the straps around her shoulders. He bent and kissed her forehead then straightened and pulled Reggie into his arms.

"Do you know how much I love you?" he asked.

"I have an idea," she said, gazing into his eyes.

"I'm thinking we're about the luckiest folks on the planet." He tilted his head at the twelve-passenger van Hank and Sadie had gifted them with at their wedding. "I always wanted a family. Now, I have one, and life couldn't get better."

"Oh, no?" Reggie winked.

His eyes narrowed as he stared down into her eyes. "You have that look on your face."

"What look?"

"The one you had when you told me you were pregnant." His eyes widened. "You're not, are you?"

"Not what?" she teased.

"You are!" Sam lifted her off her feet and spun her around. "You hear that?" he yelled into the van. "We're going to have a baby!"

A cheer went up from everyone in the van.

Sam set Reggie on her feet and smiled down at her. "I love you, Reggie Franklin, and the adventure we call our lives."

"I love you, too, Sam. And I wouldn't trade this menagerie for anything."

"Come on, we have a swearing in to go to. This is Abe's day. Let's celebrate!" Sam gave a loud, piercing whistle and yelled, "Grunt!"

The German Shepherd came barreling around the side of their house and made a flying leap into the side door of the van.

Sam and Reggie climbed into their huge van, with their huge family and drove into the sunrise of another day in the Crazy Mountains of Montana.

THE END

Thank you for reading SEAL Justice. The Brotherhood Protectors Series continues with Ranger Creed. Keep reading for the 1st Chapter.

.   .   .

Interested in more military romance stories? Subscribe to my newsletter and receive the Military Heroes Box Set

https://dl.bookfunnel.com/tug00n7mgd

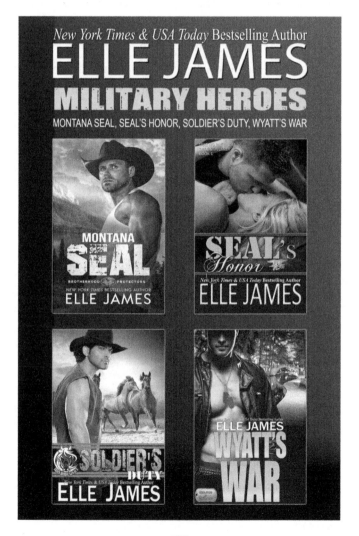

Visit ellejames.com for more titles and release dates
For hot cowboys, visit her alter ego Myla Jackson at
mylajackson.com
and join Elle James and Myla Jackson's Newsletter at
http://ellejames.com/ElleContact.htm

RANGER CREED

BROTHERHOOD PROTECTORS BOOK #14

New York Times & USA Today
Bestselling Author

ELLE JAMES

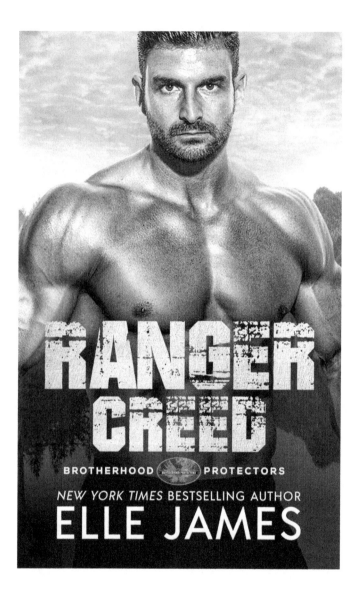

RANGER CREED

BROTHERHOOD PROTECTORS

NEW YORK TIMES BESTSELLING AUTHOR

ELLE JAMES

CHAPTER 1

"Running Bear, you copy?" Christina Samson, sitting at dispatch, asked.

Lani Running Bear keyed the mic on her radio. "I copy."

"We just received a call from Mattie Lightfoot. She needs you out at her place on Willow Creek ASAP."

Lani sighed. On her thirteenth hour of a twelve-hour shift, she was tired and ready to call it a night. Or, in this case, a morning. "Roger," she said, and turned her Blackfeet Law Enforcement Service vehicle around in the middle of the road and headed back the direction she'd come while on her way in for shift change.

Mattie Lightfoot lived in a mobile home next to Willow Creek with her grandson, Tyler. She'd raised Tyler since he was four years old, when his mother left the reservation to go make her fortune in Vegas. Her daughter, Stella Lightfoot, hadn't known who Tyler's father was. None of the men she'd slept with claimed him. Mattie's daughter had promised to send for Tyler when she'd made enough money to support them both.

Stella never sent for Tyler. She never came back to visit her son and, after a couple of years, she quit calling.

Mattie did what she could for Tyler. She worked at a convenience store in Browning, bringing in just enough money to pay utilities and groceries. Food stamps and food pantries had become a necessity. She made sure Tyler had food, even when she didn't.

A fiercely proud Blackfeet matriarch, Mattie was a respected member of the tribe. When she called for help, it was something very serious.

Lani could have refused the call and let the tribal police officer from the next shift take it. But, when she'd sworn in, she'd promised to respect and look out for members of her tribe, her family.

The drive to Mattie's place took fifteen minutes, traveling on a number of different gravel roads, until Lani finally turned onto the rutted path leading to Mattie's single-wide mobile home.

Several vehicles were parked in the yard next to Mattie's old red and white Ford pickup with the rusted wheel wells and bald tires.

Recognizing the new charcoal gray Denali, a full-sized SUV belonging to tribal elder Raymond Swift-water, Lani tensed. In her opinion, Swiftwater was a pompous ass, full of his own self-importance. He liked to think he could make decisions for the entire tribe without consulting the other elders. And he bullied the others who were older and wiser than he was into agreeing with his way of thinking.

The man was accompanied by Stanley and Stewart Spotted Dog, his minions and the muscle he kept close for intimidation purposes. Stan and Stew had broad shoulders and thick necks and arms. They were effective visual deterrents, and strong enough to take down anyone who bothered their boss.

Swiftwater crossed his arms over his chest. "About time tribal police showed up."

Lani ignored the man and walked toward the trailer. "Where's Mattie?"

"Inside," Ray said. "It ain't good. Sure you have the stomach for it?"

Since she didn't know what *it* was, she couldn't say. Instead, she walked past Swiftwater, climbed the rickety stairs and knocked on the door. "Mattie, it's me, Lani Running Bear."

A woman's sob sounded from inside. "He's gone. My boy is gone."

Lani frowned, her chest constricting at the despair in the older woman's voice. "Mattie, may I come in?"

"Door's open," Mattie said, her voice muffled.

Lani entered through the narrow door into the dark interior of a mobile home that had seen more moons than Lani had been on this earth.

Mattie Lightfoot was on the floor beside the inert body of her grandson, Tyler. He lay on his back, his face smashed, his arms battered, his chest and belly slashed by what appeared to be multiple knife wounds.

Lani's chest tightened. She'd liked the kid. He'd been going somewhere. Tyler had been committed to completing his degree and getting on with his life as soon as he could. But mostly, he'd been kind to everyone and never had anything bad to say about anyone, Native American or otherwise.

Mattie stroked Tyler's long, thick, black hair back from his forehead, tears streaming down her face as she rocked back and forth. "He's gone."

Lani didn't have to touch the base of his throat to know she'd find no pulse, but she did anyway. As she suspected, his skin was already cool to the touch, and no amount of searching would produce a pulse. "What happened, Mattie?" she asked softly.

Mattie closed her eyes and rocked. "I don't know. I don't know who could have done this to my Tyler."

Lani hated asking questions of the woman when she was deeply distressed. But she had to know as much as possible to help find who'd beaten the poor kid to death. "Did you find him here? Or did someone bring him here like this?"

"He was here when I came home from work," Mattie said. "I should have been here for him. Maybe none of this would have happened. If I'd been home, he wouldn't be dead."

"You don't know that. You could have been hurt as well."

"Rather me than him," Mattie said. "He had so much to live for."

Lani glanced around the interior of the single-wide mobile home. Though it was old, Mattie kept it clean. A mismatch of dishes was stacked neatly on a drainboard by the sink. Laundry lay neatly folded on the built-in couch. There was no blood pooling beneath Tyler's body, nor was there any broken glass or furniture in the vicinity of the body. The young man had been beaten and stabbed multiple times.

The crime hadn't been committed inside the trailer, which meant whoever had killed him had brought him there.

"Did you see anyone leaving your yard?"

Again, Mattie shook her head. "No one was here when I got home, and I didn't pass anyone on the road coming in." She stared at her grandson. "Who would have done this to Tyler? He was such a good boy."

"I'm sorry, Mattie. I don't know who did this, but I will find out. We'll find who did this to Tyler." She hoped she wasn't lying. Too often, crimes on the rez remained unsolved. "Mattie, the FBI will be involved in solving this crime. They have a lot of resources at their disposal that our own tribal police don't. They'll likely perform an autopsy and determine what weapons were used and what was the actual time of Tyler's death."

"Good. I want you to use whatever means possible to find Tyler's killer and bring him to justice."

Lani nodded. "When was the last time you saw Tyler...alive?"

Mattie's eyes filled with tears. "Yesterday afternoon. I had the night shift at the convenience store."

"Was he planning on going anywhere after dinner? Meeting anyone?"

She gave a hint of a smile. "He was going to see Natalie Preston, his girlfriend in Conrad. They had a date. He was going to take her out to the new diner for supper. He'd been working extra hours at the K Bar L Ranch so he could treat her to something special."

"Do you know if he made it to Natalie's?"

Mattie shook her head. "I had to work. I was looking forward to hearing all about their date." More tears slipped down the older woman's face.

Lani reached for Mattie's hand, squeezed it, and then pushed to her feet. "Did you call Raymond Swiftwater after you called the police?"

Mattie shook her head. "I didn't. He showed up a few minutes before you."

Lani's jaw tightened.

Swiftwater was known for showing up at reservation crime scenes.

"Could you make them leave?" Mattie asked, looking up at her.

Lani's lips pressed together in a thin line. "I'll do my best. In the meantime, I need to make some calls back at the station. I'll be back. Try not to disturb Tyler's body or any evidence. The FBI will want to look over everything very closely."

Mattie nodded and continued to stroke Tyler's hair, despite having been told not to disturb Tyler's body.

Lani left the trailer. As she descended the steps to the ground, Swiftwater approached her.

"So, what do you think?"

"I don't know what to think. A thorough investigation will have to be conducted."

"One of our people is dead," Swiftwater said. "What are you going to do about it?"

Lani squared her shoulders. "I'm going to do what I'm paid to do, and that is to investigate and find out who killed him. Now, if you'll excuse me, I need to get the FBI out here."

When she tried to go around Swiftwater, he stepped in her way, blocking her path. "Why must you call the FBI? This happened on the reservation."

"You know perfectly well the FBI has responsibility for investigating murders on the reservation."

She lifted her chin. "You know we don't have the training or the resources to conduct a thorough investigation within Blackfeet Law Enforcement Service."

Swiftwater sneered. "Then what are you good for? Writing speeding tickets and giving rides home to drunks?"

"As you are also aware, we don't have the ability to perform autopsies. We need to know the cause of death and time of death."

"I can tell you how he died," Swiftwater said. "A white man crossed onto the reservation and killed Tyler Lightfoot."

Lani planted her fists on her hips. "And you know that how? Were you there? Did you see it happen? And if you were there and saw it happen, why didn't you do something to stop it, or at least call it in?"

Swiftwater's face turned a ruddy red beneath his naturally dark skin. "We don't need an autopsy to determine what happened. It's obvious. Tyler dared to date one of their own. White men don't like it when Blackfeet date their women. Check with his girlfriend's family. I bet you'll find the murderer there."

"We'll get the FBI involved to help us find the murderer."

Swiftwater shook his head. "We don't like the FBI crawling around the reservation."

She drew a deep breath, trying to hold onto her

temper. "We don't have access to the resources available within the FBI. They have the resources and skills needed to solve this kind of crime."

Swiftwater's eyes narrowed. "And how often do they solve crimes on the reservation? I don't know why they can't leave it to our own people to solve the crimes."

Lani frowned. "You know we're always short-handed. We barely have enough staff to man two shifts."

"I've offered my own men as contract labor to help with law enforcement efforts."

She wouldn't trust Swiftwater's men any more than she'd trust Swiftwater. She suspected they were all corrupt; she just didn't have the evidence to prove it. "They aren't certified police officers. They have no authority to enforce the laws."

Lani was tired of his harassment. She narrowed her eyes. "Do you know anything about Tyler's death?"

Swiftwater blinked. "No."

"Then how did you come to be here so quickly?" she asked.

The tribal elder lifted his chin. "As a tribal elder, I have access to the police scanner. As a man responsible for the welfare of his tribe, I like to know what's happening. I also like to know how fast our law enforcement officers respond in situations such as this."

Lani snorted and turned away.

"I will report to the tribal elders how long it took you to arrive on scene."

Not bothering to reply, Lani climbed into her service vehicle, requested assistance and asked dispatch to notify the FBI.

Lani returned to the trailer to wait with Mattie. While they waited, Lani used her cellphone to take pictures of the crime scene, Tyler's body and the many wounds that had been inflicted. She knew the FBI would conduct a thorough investigation but wasn't sure they would share the information with her.

Within the hour, many of Mattie's friends and tribe women arrived in support of Mattie. At the same time, the tribal elders arrived and formed a circle around Swiftwater.

Lani, with Mattie in tow, exited the mobile home, wanting to know what the elders were discussing, and needing the older woman out of the trailer when the women converged on her. They didn't need to contaminate the crime scene any more than Mattie already had.

She found out soon enough.

"Officer Running Bear," Chief Hunting Horse called out.

Lani stepped forward. "Yes, sir."

"As the FBI will be involved in this investigation,

we want Police Chief Black Knife to be their contact. No others."

"That means you are officially off this case," Swiftwater said, stepping forward to stand beside Chief Hunting Horse.

At that moment, the chief of tribal police arrived.

Swiftwater nodded toward his vehicle. "Officer Running Bear, you can leave now."

Lani ignored Swiftwater and converged upon her head of law enforcement, Police Chief Black Knife. "Are you going to let the elders pull rank on you?"

Her boss frowned. "What are you talking about?"

"They just pulled me off this murder case."

He frowned. "What did they say?"

"That you will be the direct contact with the FBI investigation."

His frown deepened. "I'll find out what's going on." He left her standing by his vehicle and joined the tribal elders. A few minutes later, he returned, a scowl marring his forehead. "You're officially off the case."

"What? Why?" she asked.

Black Knife's face was set in stone. "There'll be no discussion. I'll see you back at the station."

When she opened her mouth to protest, he held up his hand. "No discussion."

Anger burned through her. She glanced toward the front of the mobile home where Mattie Lightfoot was being led away from the crime scene by Swiftwater.

Her gaze met Mattie's distraught one. The woman looked to her as if asking what was happening.

Lani started toward her.

A hand on her arm stopped her.

"You're off the case," Police Chief Black Knife reminded her.

"I just want to help Mattie."

"Go home. Your shift has ended." The stern look he gave her ended her arguments.

She wanted to go to Mattie and reassure her that she'd do everything in her power to find her grandson's killer, but she couldn't.

Maybe she couldn't do anything in an official capacity, but she could do something in an unofficial capacity, and she had an idea of who she could get to help her.

Lani took her service vehicle back to the station, climbed into her Jeep and headed to her cottage at the edge of the reservation. She hadn't gone five miles along the road home before a massive lump in the road forced her to slow to a complete stop.

She stared at the lump for a moment before her heart dropped to the pit of her belly. She pulled her service weapon out of her shoulder holster and stepped out of her vehicle, searching the roadside and ditches for any sign of movement. Nothing moved, including the lump in front of her.

She knew before she reached it what it was. The question wasn't so much what it was, but who.

Dressed in a gray hooded sweatshirt and sweatpants, the victim lay on one side, facing away from Lani. Her police training had her estimating height and weight. Based on how long the body was, it was either a man or a very tall woman.

As she rounded the body, she gasped. The man's face had been so badly beaten that she couldn't tell who it was. And just like Tyler, he'd been stabbed multiple times in the chest and abdomen.

Lani checked for a pulse. For a long moment, she rested her fingers on his battered neck, hoping she might find a pulse. When she finally gave up, she started to pull her hand away.

The man's body jerked, his hand came out and grabbed her wrist.

Shocked, Lani tried to pull away, but his grip was so strong, she couldn't break free.

The man's eyes opened, and he stared at her through quickly swelling eyes, his pupils dilated. "Hep ma," he groaned.

Lani forced herself to calm. The man was still alive, but for how long? "Who did this to you?"

The man made a sound like a hiss then collapsed back to the ground. His grip relaxed on her wrist, his hand falling to the ground.

Lani checked again for a pulse. Nothing. She

searched his pockets for some form of identification but found none.

She hurried back to her SUV, pulled out her handheld radio and called dispatch. "Need an ambulance ASAP." She gave the location and information on the victim. Within minutes, the Blackfeet Emergency Medical Service arrived.

They were unable to revive the victim before loading him into the ambulance.

By that time, Police Chief Black Knife arrived, along with Swiftwater and his minions.

The chief listened to her account and made notes. When she'd finished, he tipped his head toward her SUV. "You can go now."

"Sir, with all due respect, I need to be there when the FBI does their investigation."

He shook his head. "You heard the elders. I'll be the only contact for this investigation. You're off duty. Go get some rest."

Lani snorted. "Two bodies in less than twenty-four hours. You think I'm going to rest? Do you even know who that man is?"

He nodded. "It was Ben Wolf Paw."

"Ben?" Lani's heart contracted. "Ben's one of the nicest guys on the reservation. Why?"

"I don't know, but we'll figure it out." He gripped her arm. "In the meantime, I need you to take a few days off."

She frowned. "Are you kidding me? Why?

"This has been a lot for you."

She frowned. What the hell was going on? Why were they freezing her out? "I've seen worse in Afghanistan. You can't put me on leave."

"I can, and I will." He gave her stern look. "Take the leave, or I'll have to fire you." He turned and left, not giving her an opportunity to argue.

Lani stood for a long moment after the ambulance left and everyone else cleared out. She stared at the place Ben had been lying on the road.

No blood. He'd been dumped after he'd been beaten and stabbed. Had he been murdered in the same location as Tyler, and then dumped here?

She didn't have the answers and, if the police chief had his way, she wouldn't get them.

Bullshit on that. She couldn't take a few days off and not do anything. Someone was killing good people on the reservation. And she intended to keep her promise to Mattie. These murders would not be left like so many on the reservation—unsolved. Not when she could do something about it.

As soon as she reached her cottage, she called an acquaintance she'd known from her days in the Army, Zachariah Jones. Though they'd butted heads while deployed at the same base in Afghanistan, they'd had enough in common to want to keep in touch.

Zach had just left the Army and come back to his home state of Montana. He'd taken a job with a man from Eagle Rock, Montana. A man who provided security services. What she needed now was someone who would have her back while she conducted her own investigation regarding what was happening on the reservation. She needed someone who could live with her on the reservation. Someone who was a member of the Blackfeet tribe.

Zach was her man.

ABOUT THE AUTHOR

ELLE JAMES also writing as MYLA JACKSON is a *New York Times* and *USA Today* Bestselling author of books including cowboys, intrigues and paranormal adventures that keep her readers on the edges of their seats. When she's not at her computer, she's traveling, snow skiing, boating, or riding her ATV, dreaming up new stories. Learn more about Elle James at www.ellejames.com

Website | Facebook | Twitter | GoodReads | Newsletter | BookBub | Amazon

Or visit her alter ego Myla Jackson at mylajackson.com
Website | Facebook | Twitter | Newsletter

Follow Me!
www.ellejames.com
ellejamesauthor@gmail.com

ALSO BY ELLE JAMES

Shadow Assassin

Murdock (#8)

Utah (#9)

Judge (#10)

The Outriders

Homicide at Whiskey Gulch (#1)

Hideout at Whiskey Gulch (#2)

Held Hostage at Whiskey Gulch (#3)

Setup at Whiskey Gulch (#4)

Missing Witness at Whiskey Gulch (#5)

Cowboy Justice at Whiskey Gulch (#6)

Hellfire Series

Hellfire, Texas (#1)

Justice Burning (#2)

Smoldering Desire (#3)

Hellfire in High Heels (#4)

Playing With Fire (#5)

Up in Flames (#6)

Total Meltdown (#7)

Declan's Defenders

Marine Force Recon (#1)

Show of Force (#2)

Full Force (#3)

Driving Force (#4)

Tactical Force (#5)

Disruptive Force (#6)

Mission: Six

One Intrepid SEAL

Two Dauntless Hearts

Three Courageous Words

Four Relentless Days

Five Ways to Surrender

Six Minutes to Midnight

Hearts & Heroes Series

Wyatt's War (#1)

Mack's Witness (#2)

Ronin's Return (#3)

Sam's Surrender (#4)

Take No Prisoners Series

SEAL's Honor (#1)

SEAL'S Desire (#2)

SEAL's Embrace (#3)

SEAL's Obsession (#4)

SEAL's Proposal (#5)

SEAL's Seduction (#6)

Alaskan Fantasy

Boys Behaving Badly Anthologies

Rogues (#1)

Blue Collar (#2)

Pirates (#3)

Stranded (#4)

First Responder (#5)

Blown Away

Warrior's Conquest

Enslaved by the Viking Short Story

Conquests

Smokin' Hot Firemen

Protecting the Colton Bride

Protecting the Colton Bride & Colton's Cowboy Code

Heir to Murder

Secret Service Rescue

High Octane Heroes

Haunted

Engaged with the Boss

Cowboy Brigade

Time Raiders: The Whisper

Bundle of Trouble

Killer Body

Operation XOXO

An Unexpected Clue

Baby Bling

Under Suspicion, With Child

Texas-Size Secrets

Cowboy Sanctuary

Lakota Baby

Dakota Meltdown

Beneath the Texas Moon